Frankie & Lexi 3

Luvin' A Young Beast

Tina J

Copyright 2018

More Books by Tina J

A Thin Line Between Me & My Thug 1-2
I Got Luv for My Shawty 1-2
Kharis and Caleb: A Different kind of Love 1-2
Loving You is a Battle 1-3
Violet and the Connect 1-3
You Complete Me
Love Will Lead You Back
This Thing Called Love
Are We in This Together 1-3
Shawty Down to Ride For a Boss 1-3
When a Boss Falls in Love 1-3
Let Me Be The One 1-2
We Got That Forever Love
Ain't No Savage Like The One I got 1-2
A Queen & Hustla 1-2 (collab)
Thirsty for a Bad Boy 1-2
Hasaan and Serena: An Unforgettable Love 1-2
We Both End Up With Scars
Caught up Luvin a beast 1-3
A Street King & his Shawty 1-2
I Fell for the Wrong Bad Boy 1-2 (collab)
Addicted to Loving a Boss 1-3
All Eyes on the Crown 1-3
I Need that Gangsta Love 1-2 (collab)
Still Luvin' a Beast 1-2
Creepin' With The Plug 1-2
I Wanna Love You 1-2
Her Man, His Savage 1-2
When She's Bad, I'm Badder 1-3
Marco & Rakia 1-3
Feenin' for a Real One 1-3
A Kingpin's Dynasty 1-3
What Kind Of Love Is This?
Frankie & Lexi

Lexi

I woke up this morning excited about attending the doctor's appointment. Ever since Frankie and I discussed it last week, we've both been extra happy. And let's not forget that even if I weren't last week, I most likely am this week.

The two of us been staying at the hotel so we could be alone. It's fun staying at my parents, his parents and my brothers place but we wanted alone time. Walking around naked and laying up the way we used to at home is all I want and if it has to be in this hotel, then so be it. The hotel is very nice and it's where SJ's been staying when he's not at my aunt's house so I see Dree and lil man here too sometimes.

I got out the shower and picked my phone up. It was my mom asking what time I'm coming to get her. She is as excited as we are and refuses to miss the first appointment. It's funny because I'm only going to my gynecologist. But like Frankie, she insists I'm pregnant and since this is gonna be the first grand baby, she wants to be there.

I sent her a text telling her I'll be there when I'm dressed. I put the phone on the nightstand, threw my clothes on and went down the small staircase. The smell of food invaded my nostrils. I followed it and saw Frankie sitting on the couch with my brother playing that stupid Fortnite game. I was so over it, that when the system went down to update for three hours I was in my glory. Him and a bunch of other people around the world seemed to be pissed but if you have anyone in your family who plays this game, anytime it shuts down, be happy.

"Which one is mine?" I asked and got no answer. I walked over and stood in front of the television.

"Which food container is mine?" Frankie licked his lips while my brother sucked his teeth.

"You can have whatever you want. Damn, you sexy. Come here." I moved closer and he stood.

"I want you." He dropped the remote on the seat and had my hand in his.

"After the doctors Frankie." He stopped and looked at me.

6

"I promise to suck that dick so good, you'll be ready for a nap."

"Now how am I supposed to go on with the rest of my day after hearing that?"

"Because you know your fiancé is the shit and if I say something, I'm gonna do it." I lifted the lid on one of the containers and placed a piece of bacon in my mouth.

"You coming to the doctors, right?" He leaned in to kiss me.

"Yea. I'll be there." We were gonna drive together but as you can see, he's stuck on the damn game.

"Let me go get my mom and I'll see you soon. Oh and Frankie." He was on his way back to play the game.

"Make sure you drop him off. He doesn't like to hear us moaning." We both busted out laughing.

"I swear to God Lexi, you better go head." Kane, like any sibling hated to hear anything about sex regarding me. I get a kick outta bothering him though.

"Love you brother." I blew him a kiss.

"LEXI!" Frankie shouted when I opened the door.

"Yes baby."

"Stop tryna outrun the security." I busted out laughing. Him and my family were so worried about Rome finding me, they hired security to watch me. A few times I tried to shake him but it was no use because he was on it. When he told them, they were all mad at me.

"Alright."

"Lexi."

"I heard you Frankie." I closed the door and left. I'm not gonna try and lose them today anyway. My mom is still moving slow and my father and brother would kill me if I did.

****

"Well Ms. Anderson. You are indeed pregnant." The doctor said after they tested my urine

"YES!" Frankie shouted and my mom smiled.

"Would you like to see how far along you are?"

"Yup." I didn't have to open my mouth because him and my mom answered every question. The nurse brought in the machine and come to find out, I'm going on two weeks.

"Damn, I got you pregnant the same day your cast came off." My mom sucked her teeth.

"My bad, Mrs. April." He started laughing. The doctor showed our baby on the machine and allowed us to hear the heartbeat. Frankie's crazy ass had the nerve to ask if he could tell what we were having.

"Sorry, we won't know that until she's at least four or five months." He was disappointed but told him he'd pay extra to check every month.

"I'm so fucking happy Lexi." He hugged me tight. My mom was in the hallway on the phone telling my dad. She was already trying to baby shop.

"I am too. I love you." We started kissing.

"Alright you two. I'm hungry." My mom said.

"You coming?"

"Nah, I got some things to handle. I'll see you at home." He kissed my cheek and walked us outside.

"Where you wanna eat?"

"Anywhere honey." My dad called again to say congratulations and check on us. They were so overprotective and I thought it would bother me but it doesn't.

I pulled up at TGIF Friday's and helped my mom get out. She walked slow but I have no problem helping her. I opened the door and waited for the lady to seat us.

"I'm happy you and Frankie got it together." My mom smiled looking over the menu. Everyone wanted us married with kids already.

When I showed her my ring, she cried. My father said it was about time and I never should've wasted my energy on anyone else knowing Frankie is the man I wanted. I tried to explain he had someone else too but like he said, he was buying time with the ho. My mom told him to stop saying that and he'd just wave her off.

"Me too ma. I'm not sure if I wanna wait until after the baby or hurry up and get it over with since we've waited so long."

"It's whatever you want Lexi. We all know that man will walk down the aisle with you tomorrow if you want." I put my head down grinning. Frankie would drop everything to do just that.

"Are you ladies ready to order?" The waitress asked and disappeared to put it in.

My mom and I stayed in the restaurant for almost two hours eating and talking. Frankie and my dad were having a fit because they had no idea why it took us so long. They said if we weren't home soon, one of them was coming to get us.

"I'll be right back Lexi." My mom stood.

"Where you going?"

"The bathroom."

"You want me to come with you?"

"No, it's ok. Here's the money for the food and make sure your dads food is right. I don't wanna hear his mouth." We ordered for him and my siblings. Frankie ate already but I still brought food home in case. I walked up to the register, grabbed the bags and waited for my receipt. I had my head down and looked up to see my mom returning from the bathroom. The look on her face told me something wasn't right and when the person popped up behind her, I knew then shit was about go left.

The lady handed me the receipt and stepped away from the register. I left everything on the counter and went to my mother. I'm pregnant and definitely shouldn't be fighting but this motherfucker is about to make me show how my hands work.

"I don't care which one of you do it, or how you get it. But what I do know is, you got twenty minutes to call your father and tell him to bring me ten million dollars or not only is this bitch dead, but the cops will find out what happened in that hospital room." My mouth hung open. How the fuck did anyone know about my grandmother? No one was in the room with us.

"Nineteen minutes and counting." It wasn't until we stepped out the door that I noticed the gun behind my mother's back. Outta nowhere a car sped in the parking lot and stopped directly in front of us. The windows were tinted so we couldn't see inside. But when the doors opened my heart stopped and my mom reached for me. How did he find me?

SJ

"I'll be back in a few Dree and lil man, make sure you ready for me on the game." He balled his fist up and pushed it against mine.

They been staying with me off and on until I get a new place. It's fun and I couldn't for the life of me understand how a man didn't make time to spend with their seed. Not only is he smart for a kid who just turned five but he was well mannered. He also knew his limit when it came to his mom and you could tell how much he loved her.

"Got it. Bye SJ." He hopped out and ran in the house.

"SJ, please be careful." Dree stared at me with those big brown eyes. She knew Whitney contacted me about an hour ago asking if we could meet up. Dree didn't want me to go because she felt it was another set up but I had something for her ass if it was.

"I'm not leaving you baby." I pulled her closer and gently kissed her.

"Call someone else to go with you."

"Dree, I love how concerned you are but I got this."

"Fuck that. I'm coming." She pouted and folded her arms across her chest. I stepped out, went to her side and carried her in the house. She ain't about to punk me the way she did Herb. And I would never allow her in harm's way.

"What happened to her?" I heard her mom shout and come running over. By the looks of it, you would think the same way. Dree was holding my neck extra tight and telling me no, she wasn't letting go. Her pops came in the room and nodded.

"She good."

"Then what's all this for?"

"J, you know your daughter extra when he leaves." She sucked her teeth as I laid Dree on the couch.

"SJ."

"I'll be fine Dree." She kept shaking her head no. I loved this woman with all my heart but I'll never go if I stayed here.

"I'm out." Her brother Dreek said coming outta the back. We spoke and he disappeared.

14

"Am I missing something?" Her mom asked.

"Not that I know of." I said and backed away from my girl before she wrapped her arms around me again. I understood her concern and it was killing me to see her so upset but I had to get this bitch and she knew it.

"I'll be back Dree."

"SJ!" She shouted.

"Make sure you feed my baby." Her father locked eyes with me and closed the door.

I ran to my truck, typed in the destination Whitney gave me that was an hour away and sparked a blunt. I needed to be calm. I wasn't gonna smoke the whole thing because I had to be alert too in case shit goes left. There's no telling what Whitney has up her sleeve and if I know her, she'll definitely wanna fuck too.

I never told Dree about the messages she sent me. Even after the fiasco at the hospital when she tased my girl, she was still trying. I mean she sent explicit text messages along with video ones. Then, she had a few of her crying and telling me how much she loved me and if I didn't play with her heart, she would've never tried to kill me. I also got some threatening ones, which I kept so when I do take her life, shit is justified. Say what you want, but I like to keep my track record clean.

I pulled up at the house and her car was the only one there. It didn't mean shit but I'll give her the benefit of the doubt. I cut the truck off, sent her a message saying I was outside and grabbed the small carry bag I had. It had the items in it I needed and I'm sure it won't be enough time to run back and get it out. I glanced around the spot and it appeared to be a quiet area but I'm not from this spot so I had no idea if it were or not. There were no houses around and it made my reason for coming here even better.

"Hey baby." She had on one of those negligee things. This time my dick didn't get hard.

"What up?" I stepped in the door and she had some romantic shit going on. Candles, music and all that. I stood at the kitchen staring at the food she cooked. This bitch reminded me of Lynn Whitfield in, A Thin Line Between Love and Hate. It's like no matter what I said about us being over, she wasn't getting.

16

"SJ, let me start off by saying I apologize for everything. I just wanted us to be together." She wrapped her arms around my neck.

"It's all good. What you cook?" I moved her arms and checked the pots. I looked on the side of the sugar jar and noticed a small vial. She has to be the stupidest bitch I know. Who tries to drug someone and leaves the evidence out in the open?

"I made you some steak, potatoes and green beans." I admit it smelled good and whether I saw the vial or not, I wouldn't eat it.

"Where's the bathroom?" She pointed upstairs. I still had my bag on my side and took it up with me.

Instead of going in the bathroom, I went in the bedroom and this bitch had handcuffs and toys in here. I guess she had big plans for us. Too bad, Dree and I do way more shit to each other and it's much better.

I dumped the stuff out and prepared it all to make sure everything was perfect. It's not going to look like an accident but it will when I place this suicide note here. I typed it up and

17

forged her signature. I saw her sign shit a million times and even though it ain't perfect, what I did was close enough.

"YO, WHITNEY. COME HERE." I shouted at the top of the steps. She sashayed her ass up and made sure to switch the entire way. I smiled and escorted her in.

"I see you has shit set up for us." I pointed to the handcuffs in my hand.

"I did." She ran her hands up my chest.

"How about we skip dinner and start now?" She removed the thin robe and I pushed her on the bed.

"Let's start with these cuffs." She smiled and allowed me to put them on her with no questions asked. It was now clear as day, that she was in love with me. I mean who would let a man do this knowing he said he was gonna kill you?

"I missed you so much baby." She opened her legs and stared at me. I pretended to unbuckled my jeans.

"Give it to me baby."

"Close your eyes while I pour this massage oil on you." She did like I asked.

I placed the gloves on my hand and grabbed the small can of gasoline. It was in one of those small paint cans you get from Home Depot. I had it in a freezer bag zipped up to keep the smell down.

I poured it on her legs slowly to give it the feeling of being lotion. It didn't take long for her to notice the difference.

"Why does it smell like gasoline?"

"Because I'm about to set yo ass on fire." Her eyes popped open. I only planned on giving her a bullet to her head but once Frankie told me what he did to Crystal. I felt it was only fair to make her feel what would've happened to me if she succeeded with the cocktail and if I got caught in the house when she tried it burn it down.

"SJ, please take these handcuffs off me." She was squirming, wiggling and doing any and everything tryna get out.

"Nah. You said, you missed me and wanted to fuck."

"SJ, stop playing." I took my gun out and shot her in the leg. Her scream only intensified the pleasure I received seeing her in pain. Tears were flooding her face and blood began to pour out.

"I'm gonna let you feel what I would've felt when you tried to burn me alive. The shot is for whoever helped you that night but trust, I'm gonna get that motherfucker too." I flipped the lighter.

"SJ, please." She cried out.

"Remember you set my house on fire while I slept?" She didn't say anything.

"Have fun with Crystal and save room for everyone who helped you." I let the flame touch the comforter and watched as the fire overtook her body. Watching her flesh burn is pretty nasty and I didn't feel bad. I couldn't because had I not shot through the windshield, it would've been me.

Once the room engulfed in flames, I let the rest of the gasoline fall on the rug until it ran out. It's just a matter of time before the entire house burned. And because this house is in a secluded area, it would take a while for someone to report it.

I made sure I had everything and placed the suicide letter under a rock close to the house. It was in a red envelope so it won't be missed when the cops came on the property. I walked to my truck and had this aching feeling that something was wrong with Lexi. I pulled my phone out to call her but something or should I say someone, stopped me.

"What's up now nigga?" I felt the steel on the back of my head.

"Herb?" I questioned.

"Damn right it's me. How's it feel to know I'm about to take your life, for ruining mine?" I heard the gun cock.

Did I really let this cornball catch me slipping?

Raya

"You ready ma?" Kane asked and carried me to the car. I had a doctor's appointment to see if my arm and leg healed. I prayed they did because this carrying me shit was getting on my nerves. I wanted to walk and have sex with my man, who refused until I had at least one cast off. I can't even lie; I've tried many times and he will not budge. Talking about he likes to do a lot and he ain't got time to hear me complaining.

"Yea. I can't wait to get these casts off."

"Me too. I love the way you give me head but I need to feel inside."

"And I can't wait for you to do it." He bit down on his lip and I all I wanted was for him to lay me down and make love to me.

"Let's get you to the doctor." He lifted and carried me to the truck. After he placed the seatbelt on, he locked his house up and jumped in the driver's side.

"Ima need you to ride the fuck outta me when you get this leg cast off." He squeezed my upper thigh and drove off. I couldn't help but laugh. He was definitely a piece of work, said whatever is on his mind and yet; I was deeply and irrevocably in love with him.

It could be his bluntness or sexiness. Whatever the case, he's all mine and now that my parents know about him, I'm showing him off any chance I get.

"Yea, I'll be there when I finish at the doctors with Raya." I heard Kane say on the phone. He hung up and pulled in the parking lot at the office.

He went inside, retrieved a wheelchair and returned with a smile on his face. I opened the door with my good hand and for some reason felt as if someone were watching me. The feeling was so strong, it made me scared about getting out.

"What's wrong?" I surveyed the parking lot and no one was there.

"Nothing. I'm ok." I gave him a smile and waited for him to place me in the chair. The closer we got to the door, the feeling went away.

"You sure?"

"Yea. Oh and if you need to leave, it's ok."

"Nah, it was my mother. She wants to see me."

"Go head baby. My mom is meeting me here so I won't be alone."

"It's fine Raya." His phone started ringing again.

"Kane, no one knows I'm here. I'll be fine baby."

"You tryna get rid of me?" I laughed and told him no. I know his mom is still recovering and he was a mama's boy. I didn't wanna be the girlfriend who kept him away from his family.

"You sure?" He asked when I told him again to go check on her.

"Yea. My mom just sent a text saying she's on her way." I showed her message to him and he seemed to be ok.

"Aight. Call me when you're finished." He kissed my lips and walked out. The minute he did, the eerie feeling of someone watching me returned. No one came in after us so I wasn't sure as to why.

I waited for the nurse to call my name. Once she did, she came out and pushed me to the back. There were others in the rooms and I couldn't help but wonder where my mom was.

Knowing her, she stopped to grab a coffee or something. I sent her a text when the nurse left the room. She said she wasn't coming because she figured Kane was there.

"Ma, I told Kane it was ok to leave because you were coming." I said to my mom on the phone when I called her.

"I'm sorry honey. Your dad wanted to go out for lunch. Do you want us to come?"

"No. I'll send Kane a message to come back." We conversed for a few more minutes and hung up. I hurried to call Kane because something was off. He didn't answer and it made me worry. I called back three more times.

"Hey, Ms. Hollis." The doctor said and started his exam.

By the time he finished, an hour had passed and the cast on my leg was removed and he placed a smaller one on my arm. I was so excited because I could walk and do things on my own. He said one of the nurses would return with all my paperwork and new appointment date. I started to text Kane to see if he was in the waiting room when the door opened. I looked up expecting to see the doctor but this man was far from that.

"What are you doing here?" I looked back down at my phone to send the message but he snatched the phone out my hand. I hadn't seen him in a while and he shows up here taking my shit. Who the hell did he think he was?

"What you mean why am I here? I'm always around." He locked the door and moved closer. I didn't even know these offices had locks.

"Excuse me!"

"Raya, don't act like we don't have history." He had his hand on my face.

"MOVE!" His hands were now on the side of the chair with his face about to touch mine.

"How could you sleep with that nigga? I was supposed to be your first. Then you dressed sexy and performed for him." My entire body froze when he said that.

"Have you... Have you been watching me?" I was scared for the answer but needed to hear it.

"I've been watching you for a very long time Raya."

Kane Jr.

"Ma, where you at?" I yelled throughout the house. She called me a while ago asking to see me. I was gonna wait until Raya finished at the doctors because I didn't wanna leave her alone but once she showed me the message from her mom, I felt a little better. Plus, ain't nobody gonna bother her there.

"What the fuck you yelling for punk?" My dad came out the basement with red eyes.

"Ma sent me a text saying she wanted to see me."

"Her and Lexi went out to eat."

"Oh. A'ight then. You down to get beat in the game?" I asked.

"Nigga, you ain't said nothing but a word." My pops and I were very competitive against one another. Sometimes my mom would snatch the plug out because we'd get loud and obnoxious. He told me to give him a minute to grab something to drink.

I went to speak to my siblings and of course Mariah's nosy ass came right behind me asking where have I been. I swear she was too grown for her age sometimes.

"What Mariah?" She followed me down the stairs and stopped at the basement door.

"Is daddy, really my dad?" I stopped in my tracks and turned around to see her not only confused but with tears rolling down her face.

"POPS!" I shouted down the basement.

"What?"

"Come here real quick." I lifted my sister in my arms and wiped her face. I could've told her the truth but it'll sound better coming from him.

"What's wrong Riah?" That's what called her. She laid her head on my shoulder.

"Why she crying? You better not had took shit from her." I've been known to take any type of sweets or candy she had. She'd always tell on me and I had to hear shit from him and my mom.

He reached out and she went in his arms. When he asked her again what was wrong, she hugged him tighter and cried harder. I know my grandmother had to be the one to put it in her head that she isn't my pops. It's the only logical reason for her to question it. She lifted her head off his shoulder and stared before opening her mouth.

"Are you my real dad?" I thought he was gonna flip but he held it together. It doesn't mean he wasn't upset because his facial expression told it all.

"Mariah Anderson you are my daughter."

"Are you sure because grandma said mommy was doing things behind your back and..." All Mariah did was make me wish my grandmother was alive so I could kill her dumb ass again.

"Mariah, grandma is a very mean person. She didn't like your mom and said bad things about her all the time." She nodded.

"It's ok though because God don't like ugly and since she did those things, he took her away."

"He did?" My parents hadn't told my younger siblings about her dying. He said they didn't need to know because she wasn't around enough for them to even care.

My uncle had a small memorial service for her and he, my grandfather and a few people who knew her, were the only ones there. My aunt Essence refused to attend or allow any of my cousins to go. SJ said, his dad tried to cause a scene over it but once my aunt shut him down about it, wasn't much he could do.

"Yes, he did and I'm happy because all she did was hurt mommy."

"Why didn't God take her sooner?" He looked at me.

"Trust me, he wanted to but he gave her a chance to change." She seemed to be ok after that and ran in the living room to watch TV. The song to whatever show she liked came on and she hauled ass.

"You good?" I asked because stress was written on his face.

"Yea. What time did your mom call and ask you to come over?"

"Maybe an hour ago. Oh shit." I felt around for my phone and realized I left it in the truck.

"What?"

"My phone in the truck." I was about to go get it but remembered Raya was gonna be with her mom. When they get together, she barely texts or calls. Talking about they have woman to woman talk.

"Something's off." He said and stared at his phone.

"What you mean?"

"I spoke to your mom not too long ago and she said, her and Lexi were on their way home. It don't take that long to get here." He picked his cell up to call and my mom's phone went to voicemail repeatedly.

"FUCK! Where's Frankie?" He yelled and ran upstairs to get his keys and wallet. I picked the house phone up and dialed his number.

"Tell Lexi, I'm already on my way to get her." He answered, which let me know he had no idea either.

"Shit!"

"Kane Jr.?" He questioned. He probably wasn't expecting me to answer.

"What you doing there? I thought you were with SJ." Then it dawned on me that my cousin was about to do some dangerous shit too. I forgot about him going to see Whitney. We all knew she was supposedly head over heels for him; yet, she tried to kill him and Dree.

"I came to see my mom but she wasn't here. What restaurant they at?" He told me and we jumped in the truck. I didn't have time to look down at my phone to see if Lexi called because my pops was panicking.

"Yo, where the fuck are you?" He barked in his phone at security. We made sure to send those motherfuckers with them in case Rome lurked in the shadows. With his baby mama being dead, we already knew he'd be on a warpath. Whether he loved her or not, that's still his kids mother. But then again, it don't really matter because he'll be with her soon.

The drive to the spot was far as hell, and it seemed as if every old person alive was on the road. I tried to get my pops to relax but it was no use. Due to my mom and sister not answering, his patience went straight out the window. I know it's because not only is Lexi pregnant and just getting over the other attack's, but my mom isn't fully healed. She won't be able to protect herself or Lexi and I think that's what bothers us the most.

"Don't let that bitch move." He hung up and looked at me.

"What?"

"You don't wanna know." He shook his head and stared out the window.

"Tell me pops."

"You'll see when we get there." We we're literally two streets over from the spot. When we pulled in, there were four cop cars, my mom and sister were standing next to the security dude and out the corner of my eye, I noticed the Wendy bitch in the cut. What the fuck is she doing here?

"What happened?"

"I don't know but we about to find out." We heard a car screech in the parking lot and Frankie jumped out.

"What the fuck?" He ran over to us.

"Are you ok?" My dad checked them over and Frankie hugged my sister tight.

"Where's Raya?" Lexi asked.

"At the doctors. Oh shit." I ran to the truck and grabbed my phone. I had tons of missed calls from her and a message saying her mom couldn't pick her up. I called back to back and she didn't answer.

"Y'all good here?"

"What's wrong son?" My mom knew me like a book.

"Something happened to Raya."

"What?" Frankie shouted.

"I don't know for sure but I have a ton of missed calls and now she's not answering."

"That doesn't mean anything's wrong." My mom said.

"Her mom was supposed to get her from the doctors, which is why I left. The message said she couldn't and for me to come. Ma, she won't let her phone go to voicemail for me." I kissed her cheek and ran back to my truck. I sped out the parking lot, not caring about the cops.

Once I made it to the doctor's office, I went inside and asked if Raya was still there. The nurse took me in the back and for some reason the door was locked. I knocked because maybe the doctor is still in there. It doesn't explain why the door isn't opening.

"Raya? You in there?"

"Mmmm. Mmmmmm." I heard and the nurse looked as confused as me.

"Is that you Raya?" You heard the noise again and shortly after, her call my name.

"Kane, he's here." I heard a loud noise and started kicking the door. It took me a few good kicks before it finally opened.

"WHAT THE FUCK!"

Raya

"Javier, why have you been watching me?" I asked my bodyguard. He's been doing my security since I was a kid and to know he's been doing more than protecting me is disgusting.

"I didn't mean to fall in love with you. It just happened." He tried to kiss me but I turned my head.

"In love with me? How is that even possible? We've only spoken in the car about a few things, here or there but we've never interacted in anything inappropriate. And you're married with kids. What's wrong with you?" I tried to remain calm but the closer he got, the harder it was. The fact that I couldn't really move didn't help either.

"Look at me Raya." His hand gripped my chin as he forced me to stare at him.

"I knew you were off limits from day one and I swear, I never looked at you until the day you graduated." I rolled my eyes.

"I'm serious. It wasn't until that moment, I realized that you and I were meant to be."

"Javier, not only are you thirty years old and a grown ass man, you have a wife and two kids. How could you record me without my knowledge? My father trusted you, hell; I trusted you."

"I know and I'm sorry." He pressed his lips against mine and allowed his tongue to push its way into my mouth. I bit down hard as I could until the brunt from the smack he placed on my face stopped me.

"You fucking bitch." There was blood dripping from his mouth. I stood on my good leg and walked very slow to the door. Well, I thought I did but my ass was maybe a foot away from where I stood.

I felt my hair being yanked back and fell into his body. I couldn't fight him off with only the use of one leg and one arm but I damn sure tried. He lifted me on the table, ripped my shirt down the middle and snatched my bra off. I never in my life wanted to be a victim of rape but it looks like I'll be a statistic.

His mouth latched on to my neck as he held his hand over my mouth. I tried to bite down but it was no use. This man overpowered me and the only thing I could think of was to headbutt him. I did that and ended up falling back.

All of a sudden there was a light knock on the door. I tried to yell out but my voice was muffled do to Javier. He continued sucking on my chest and neck, as if no one was on the other side of the door. This man really is crazy.

"Raya?" I heard Kane and tried everything to get him to hear me. Javier punched me so hard I hit the floor. I can't tell you what happened next because all I saw was blackness.

****

"Who the fuck is that?" I heard Kane Jr. yelling and opened my eyes. I glanced around the room and noticed I was no longer in the doctor's office but in the hospital. There were a few men who appeared to be detectives standing there with a phone in their hand.

"Sir, we need you to calm down."

"Don't tell me to calm down when my fucking girl was attacked in the doctor's office."

"Kane." I said as loud as I could. He turned to see me tryna sit up and came over.

"You ok Raya?"

"Did you get him?"

"Get who?"

"Javier. Did you get him?" The detectives stared but didn't move from where they stood. I don't know if they heard me because I wasn't loud and the TV was on.

"Javier who? The only one I know is your bodyguard and no one has seen him since you been back home." He stared at me and must've figured it out. Kane never met Javier but he knew the name from me saying who he was.

"Ain't no fucking way!"

"Kane please call my father."

"He's on his way. Raya, please tell me the bodyguard isn't who's been watching you." I started crying.

"No wonder the nigga was able to get those cameras in there. He had full access to you. FUCKKKKKK!" He slammed his fist down on the hospital table.

"Ma'am do you know the guy who attacked you?" The detective asked and before I could answer my father kicked him out the room.

My mom ran over and apologized over and over. I told her it's not her fault and she couldn't have known something like that would take place. Kane still had anger written on his face and once he and my father stepped out, I knew the two of them were about to go full force looking for Javier. Kane may not know who he is but my father does and I'm sure he has tons of information on him. I feel sorry for his family because I guarantee, that's the next stop.

"Did he...?" My mom stopped herself from asking.

"Almost ma.

"What do you mean?"

"He ripped my clothes and bra off and started sucking on my breasts. Kane got there just in time and if he hadn't, I don't know what would've happened." She hugged me.

"I was so scared he would rape me. Ma, he's the one who recorded me and admitted to watching me for a long time."

"WHAT?" She screamed out and made my father run back in.

"You ok?"

"I want his family dead. I don't care how many kids he has Hurricane. Either he goes, or his family goes."

"Promise, you know I don't murder kids."

"Well then you better hurry up and find him because not only did he violate my daughter by taping her but attempting to rape her, is where I draw the line. Now." My mom stood up and moved closer to him.

"Like I said. If you don't get him soon, his family will suffer." She patted him on the face and said she'd be right back. I think she wanted my father and I to speak. He sat on the side of me.

"Your mother is crazy."

"Do you think she'll kill his family? Daddy, his wife is very nice and the kids don't have anything to do with it." He smiled and chuckled.

"Raya, your mom is very crazy when it comes to family. You don't wanna know the things she's done to keep us

42

together." I stared at him. My mom is so laid back and understanding that I don't see hatred or danger in her.

"As far as his family goes, honey he knows exactly what he signed up for. He also knows that you never fuck with my family."

"But daddy."

"I'll try not to let his actions affect his family but I can't make promises."

"I understand." I put my head back.

"What the fuck was he thinking by taping you?"

"I have no idea." I laid on my head on his shoulder.

"It makes me wonder how long he's been doing it and why you? Has he done this to other kids?" The more questions he asked, the angrier he became.

"I don't know dad. All I know is, I'm glad Kane arrived when he did."

"Shit, me too." Kane stepped in the room with anger still on his face.

"Let me go try and calm your mom down." He kissed my forehead.

"Kane, remember what we spoke about." He nodded and laid in the bed with me.

"What y'all talk about?" I turned on my side and rested my head on his chest.

"He said, not to get you pregnant for a few more years."

"What?" I sat up.

"Yea. He said, he knows I fuck the shit outta you and it's only a matter of time before. -" I cut him off.

"You lie." He busted out laughing.

"Nah, we were discussing Javier. He's gonna send me some photos of him since I don't know what he looks like."

"What you mean? Wasn't he in there when you opened the door?"

"No one was in there Raya."

"But how did he get away? He was there. I'm not making this up." Kane lifted my head and wiped my face.

"I know you're not. Evidently, there's an adjoining door that leads into another room. He must've ran through there to get out. On the video, you see him in the parking lot

44

but because he wore a hoodie, his face was hidden." He ran his hands through my hair.

"I'm gonna get him Raya and make him pay for everything."

"I believe you." I leaned in to kiss him and he stopped me.

"Did he do that?" He pointed to my eye and then my chest. There was a small red mark that appeared to be a hickey and my eye was barely opened. I just started crying.

"How far did he get?" I told him what I remembered and just like my father, his anger grew.

"You're gonna stay with me for awhile. You cool with that?" I told him yes and laid back on his chest. It didn't take me long to dose off due to the nurse coming in a few minutes ago and dispensing pain medication. All I know is, I hope they find him soon because living in fear is not how I expected my life to turn out.

Lexi

"You ok?" My dad and Frankie kept asking me and my mom. When they showed up I knew it was about to be a problem.

"We're good."

"Then why all these cops here?" My father waved his hand around the parking lot.

"Well boss. Your daughter here, did something to her phone where I couldn't track her." I gave the security dude the dirtiest look. How the hell he out here snitching?

"WHATTTTTTTT!" My father and Frankie shouted.

"I was directly behind her when she left the doctors. She made it through a light and instead of waiting for me like she usually does, I saw her speed off. I went through the light and a truck almost rear ended me. Unfortunately, it was so much traffic that I lost her. I hit the tracker and she it led me to some town an hour away." My mom looked at me.

"When I realized she wasn't there, I sped back to town. I only found her because I kept riding around and saw them coming out."

What he said was true. I learned a trick on the internet about tricking the GPS system. It was more like a scrambler and would send you outta the way. It's hard to do and I've tried a few times but it didn't work. I'm actually shocked it did yet upset because had I not done it, my stupid ass aunt wouldn't have been able to catch us slipping.

For those of you who don't know, my aunt June is probably the most hated in my family besides my grandmother. She's hateful, vindictive, manipulating and thinks the world owes her something. Her father, who is my grandfather couldn't stand her and always said, he thinks she was switched at birth. That changed over the years when he realized her and my uncle Stacy were alike in more ways than one but he still couldn't stand her.

My aunt Essence hated her because when we were kids June stayed with them. My aunt came home from work and caught her, who was twenty at the time having sex with a

47

forty-year-old man in her bed. Needless to say, Essence beat her up so bad my uncle had to take June to the hospital and pay her off to say she was jumped.

Then, my father won his case against the state of California for false imprisonment along with some other shit and put five million in an account for her. My grandmother had access to her money and from what my father said, she ran through it a long time ago. Now here she is back again, demanding ten million from my dad or she's going to the cops. It's like when one door closed and we moved on from bullshit, a lot more seemed to open.

"Why didn't you call?" My father questioned the security dude.

"I did boss. A few times and no one answered." He glance down at his phone and said there were missed calls from him and he forgot to call him back because by the time he saw them, he was already in route to us.

"Lexi, you got one more time to go play these fucking games with the security. One fucking more." My dad said and no one said a word.

48

"I don't give a fuck how much of a pain in the ass you feel they are. Do that shit again and see what happens." He stood in my face.

"Do I make myself clear?" I could tell my mom felt bad and wanted to say something but she remained quiet too. We all know not to say anything when he's this mad.

"Yes." I put my head down and Frankie took my hand in his to walk to his car.

"Where is my sister?" My dad yelled before I sat down.

"I don't know. She ran off when she heard the cops coming."

"Frankie take her home and I'll call you in a few. With my sister lurking, ain't no telling what she's up to." He nodded and closed the door.

"Frankie, I." He put his hand up.

"But. -"

"Just stop talking." I folded my arms and pouted in the seat like a big ass kid. Yes, I was wrong for sending security on a goose chase but I'm tired of them going everywhere.

Rome is probably long gone by now and they're still having people watch us.

We pulled up to the house and I noticed a huge black fence and security cameras all over. I guess he's been making changes while we were away. He pressed a code to get in and drove up to the driveway. It felt good being home and I couldn't wait to take a hot bath. After the events of today, it will definitely relax me.

There was a code to get in the house, along with the key and once he opened the door, tears flooded my eyes. Pink and blue balloons lined the living and dining room. Streamers were hanging from the ceiling and a big congratulations banner hung low from the ceiling. I turned to look at him and he was on his way up the steps. Putting my pride to the side, I made my way up there and prepared the apology in my head. It would have to be a good one to forgive the shit I pulled today.

Again, tears flooded my eyes when I saw the candles lit, heard music playing and gift bags all over the bed. I had a good man and all he's ever wanted to do is protect me but I had to overdo it.

I saw him grab a towel and head into the bathroom. I was right behind him but stopped in my tracks when he slammed the shower door, damn near shattering it. It's gonna be a long ass night.

****

"Bitch, what you do?" Dree asked when I called her after stepping out the shower. I assumed Frankie would be in the bed but he was gone. I'm not talking about in another room gone. I mean, out the house gone.

"Why you say that?"

"Lexi we been friends long enough for me to know when something's up or you did some bullshit." I blew my breath and started explaining everything, when she too went off.

"Lexi, not only are you playing with your life but you're playing with your mothers. What would've happened if your crazy ass aunt shot her? I'm not saying this to be mean but she's not fully healed yet and you on some James Bond shit."

"Whatever."

"I'm serious Lexi. I don't think your mom would've been able to handle another shooting." I let the tears come down my face. The thought of losing my mother weighed heavy on me.

"I fucked up huh?" I wiped my eyes.

"Real bad. You better hope your evil ass father lets you come over." We both started laughing.

"Where's SJ?" And just like that, her mood changed.

"I don't know Lexi."

"What you mean, you don't know?"

"He dropped me off and left. I haven't seen him. You don't feel anything bad about him, do you?"

"No why? You think he out there being reckless?"

"I can't even tell you because he doesn't wanna worry me. I know he went to see Whitney but I'm worried because she set him up the last time." That must be where Frankie went.

"My twin powers aren't detecting any harm." She laughed hard as hell. People always thought we were bugging when we said, we felt when the other was in trouble.

"He'll be fine Dree. You know he ain't about to go anywhere with you being pregnant. He's excited."

"I know and I'll be glad when he gets here. At least, I'll now he's safe." She and I spoke a little longer and I took my ass to bed. I'm not worried about Frankie cheating on me but I wish he was here.

SJ

"How I ruin your life Herb?" I asked with my back still turned. It didn't matter that he had a gun on me because he's a punk and too scared to use it. If he weren't, I wouldn't be answering his questions.

"You know how much I loved Dree." I busted out laughing.

"Nigga, you had a good woman who loved you. You couldn't protect her and cheated. Do you really believe I ruined your life?"

CLICK! When I heard the other gun, I swung around and knocked the shit outta him.

"What took yo ass so long?" I asked Dreek, who stood there with a blunt hanging out the side of his mouth.

See when Whitney contacted me, I knew I had to take someone with me for this reason right here. I wasn't quite sure who she'd bring but I knew it was someone. I brought Dreek Jr. because he's someone who stayed in the cut and only came out if you needed him. He liked it that way because in his eyes, it made people think he was a punk and that's how he wanted it. Unfortunately, his ass is almost as crazy as my cousin Kane. Now that nigga ain't got it all either.

"Man, I couldn't find this place." He kicked Herb in the ribs just because. Him and Dree are definitely something else. She did the same thing to Whitney after beating her up. Its like the two of them needed one last hit. Petty, I know.

"GPS works motherfucker." I told him and placed Herb's gun in my truck.

"Yea whatever. This shit is in the cut and we need to get the fuck outta here." We heard sirens and they were getting louder.

"Help me get him in the truck." I said. I wasn't sure if we'd come as close to this nigga again and I didn't wanna take a chance on him skipping town.

"Well get him another time."

"Dreek, I ain't leaving him."

"We don't have a choice SJ. It's either stay and get caught or leave and find him later." I finally hopped in and pulled off with Dreek behind me. The fire trucks and cops flew past us. I saw them turn at the house and laughed. The shit was almost ashes, which meant so was Whitney.

I drove to my hotel to change and they go get Dree. I still had her crying etched in my head and the only way to get it out, is to see her. She has definitely become a fixture in my life. My entire family loves her and it's vice versa when it came to hers. I mean they only told us for the last few years to fuck and get it over with. Now that we did, we've been stuck together like glue.

"Yo!" I answered my phone after hopping out the shower. My side still had some pain in it but I'm good.

"I'm about to kill your cousin." Frankie breathed heavy in the phone. He was supposed to come with me to get Herb but he couldn't find Lexi. It looks like he did and from the sounds of it, she messed up big time.

"What happened?"

"Man open the door." He hung up and I heard him knocking.

"Where yo key?" We each had keys to each other's spot.

56

"Bro, I do not wanna walk in on you and Dree fucking." I had to laugh because he almost did once. My girl heard the door close and jumped under the covers.

"She ain't here." I closed the door and told him to hold on so I could throw some clothes on.

After I finished, I went back in there to find him with his head laid on the couch, feet on the table and smoke coming out his mouth. Whenever he did this, it meant he had heavy shit on his mind. I took the blunt out his hands, sat down and waited for him to speak.

"Your cousin did some stupid shit that almost got her and your aunt killed."

"Say what?"

"Yea man." He sat up.

"How about I go out after finding out she's pregnant and buy all this shit. I'm talking congratulations balloons, and some pink and blue shit. Then I did all this romantic stuff in the bedroom."

"Spare me Frankie."

"Shut yo ass up. Do I say that when you and Dree talk about the stuff y'all get from Spencer's?"

"Ugh Yea. You usually say, don't nobody wanna hear what you do behind closed doors."

"I do, don't I?" This nigga had the nerve to say and start laughing.

"Yea."

"That's different tho."

"How nigga?"

"I don't know. Anyway. I'm waiting for her to go back to her mom's so I can pick her up when she's done. Your uncle calls and asks if I seen her, which puts me in panic mode."

"Is she ok?" I jumped up ready to go.

"Nigga sit yo ass down. You know damn well your fake ass twin antennas would've went up." I fell over laughing.

"Long story short, she did some shit to trick the GPS. Security went over to some location an hour away and by the time he found them, your crazy ass Aunt June had a damn gun in Mrs. April back." He shook his head.

"WHAT?"

"Yup. She was gone by the time we arrived but had security not gotten there in time, it's no telling what could've happened. Then she's requesting ten million dollars." I scoffed up a laugh.

"Wait! Didn't your uncle give her money?" I took a pull of the small portion of the blunt that was left.

"Hell yea he did."

I remember my mom telling me how uncle Kane gave her money and left it with his mom to monitor how she used it. Evidently, my aunt had all types of habits and one was getting high off whatever and disappearing with different men. I don't know when but she talked my grandmother into transferring the money straight to her. Within two years, her back account had depleted. She contacted my pops a few times asking for money and my mom shut it down.

To be honest, I thought the bitch was dead. I call her that because she's tried to make my dad feel bad for not giving her money, which caused complications in my parents' marriage. My mom wasn't being a bitch in my eyes. She was more or less telling my dad, if he gave her money once, after she runs out, she'll be back again and again.

Sure enough, my father went behind my mom's back and gave her some. He told her not to come around or ever mention it but my aunt couldn't stand my mom ever since she got her ass beat for fucking in their bed.

June couldn't stay away and showed up at my cousin Mariah's one-year old birthday party and shit hit the fan. My uncle Kane cursed her out for showing up unannounced. He said, she was there to be mean to April, per my grandmother. She denied it and before leaving made sure to thank my father for the money he gave her. The look on my mother's face was priceless and as usual, it took my father weeks to get back in my mom's good graces.

Now this bitch is back demanding more money. It only means more shit is about to hit the fan. I need to warn my mom before she sees her.

Frankie

When Lexi admitted to losing the security guy on purpose, all of us were furious. I don't even think her mom was aware because her facial expression told it all. I'm sure having someone following you can be annoying but there's a reason for everything.

Rome got her twice already and you would think it scared her enough to want a ton of security around but not her. She's taking the shit as a joke and for someone to be smart, she makes a lotta dumb moves.

I brought her home, took a shower and bounced without telling her. She called me a few times but I sent her to voicemail. I mean why not? If she can't keep herself safe and let someone know where she is, why should I?

After smoking and kicking it with SJ, I went to the liquor store and grabbed me a few bottles of Henney. I only drank this when I was stressed out and home. Henney will have a nigga down for the count and I'm not tryna get caught slipping.

I put the code in the gate, waited for it to close and walked to the door. I noticed Lexi in the window and all I wanted to do is make love to her but again, she pissed me off big time. I'm not being a brat or even petty but she needs to learn that motherfucker is out there waiting and won't hesitate next time to kill her or anyone else he can.

"Hey." She spoke softly when I closed the door. Instead of responding, I dropped my keys on the table and went straight in the basement.

"Not right now Lexi." She sat next to me.

"I'm sorry Frankie." I opened the Henney and took a swig.

"How can you be a smart dummy?"

"No you didn't just call me that." She could be offended all she wants but it's how she was acting. Plus, she hated when her brother said it to her, so I know it's fucking with her.

"Why not? It's how you're acting."

"How is that?" She folded her arms. I took my shirt off and kicked my sneakers to the side.

62

"Because you're smart as hell Lexi, yet; out here doing dumb shit. Like, were you even thinking about how much danger you put your mom in? What about yourself?"

"Frankie." I put my hand up.

"You have the brace off, just found out we're expecting, and your mom is still in recovery and what do you do?" I took another swig because thinking about it was pissing me off. I wanted to smoke but I wouldn't while she is in my presence due to my baby.

"You play some damn trick on the security and end up with your aunt putting a gun in your mom's back." She put her head down.

"What if he didn't get there? Huh? What if your mom made one wrong move and June shot her? I know it would've been devastating for the family but do you know what it would've done to your father? Do you even care how your actions are affecting all of us?" She sat there crying and I didn't feel bad at all. This is the second time I had to address her behavior. I let it slide the first time but I couldn't do it this time. She needed to hear it.

Instead of listening to her cry, I took my ass upstairs because I may give in and apologize myself for being mean and that wouldn't make shit better. It will only teach her crying will make me give in and I can't have that. I will say it again though, Lexi needs to know her actions are affecting everyone whether she wants to believe it or not. Then I go outta my way to surprise her and for what? Hell yea, I'm taking my ass to bed. She can cry all night if she wants.

****

"Got damn Lexi. Shit!" I moaned out when she put both of my balls in her mouth. I guess after four days of not speaking, this is how she'd get my attention and she's right. Waking me up like this will definitely get it.

"Fuck, I'm gonna nut Lexi." She took that as a message to suck and jerk me harder and faster.

"Ahhh shit." I gripped the back of her hair and my hands fell to the side when she drained me of everything I had. My ass was breathing heavy and ready to go back to sleep.

"I'm sorry baby. I promise never to let it happen again." Her lips were on mine and her tongue played its own game in my mouth. Once my dick woke up, she used one of her hands to guide him inside. Thank goodness she gave me head first because I damn sure would've cum quick.

"You forgive me?" She leaned back, placed her hands on the front part of my legs and rode the fuck outta me. I ain't even gonna lie, Lexi had my eyes rolling, toes curling and she would've definitely gotten pregnant.

"I'm cummin Frankie. Oh Goddddd. Shittttt." She screamed out and fell face forward on my chest. I didn't give her time to recuperate and flipped her over. I was gentle due to her recent injuries but I wasn't gentle inside that good ass pussy.

"Fuck Frankie." Both of her hands gripped the sheets as she threw her ass back.

"Don't do that shit again." I hit her with a stroke so deep she almost jumped off the bed.

"I won't. I'm cumming againnnnnn." Her body shook, ass jiggled and she fell forward. Well tried, because I laid on the side, lifted her leg, plunged inside and continued fucking the shit outta her. Oh she's gonna remember not to do it again.

"I love you Frankie." She moved my arm to her belly and kissed the top of my hand after we finished.

"I love you too." I kissed her shoulder blade and dosed off right behind her. Good sex, no amazing and make up sex will do that to you.

****

"Do you have any idea where that nigga can be?" Kane Jr. asked about Javier. I knew he was Raya's bodyguard for years but I didn't really know him like that.

"Nah. My uncle is trying not to go by his house because he doesn't murder kids and didn't really wanna take it out in his wife, but each day he's missing, its making it harder."

"Hell yea. He has to know Raya told us."

"I'm sure he does, which is exactly why he hasn't been seen. Look at this nigga." I pointed to SJ coming out Dree's house. She had her hands wrapped around his neck and the two of them started going at it like we weren't in the fucking car waiting. Kane reached over and blew the horn a few times. He didn't toot it either. That nigga kept his hand on it just to be annoying. Dree stuck her finger up and closed the door behind her.

"Damn, nigga I know you gave her enough last night. Tha fuck!" Kane said when SJ plopped in the backseat.

"Bro, she missed me and of course I had to give her what she wanted before leaving. You know make her hurt as she walks so she can feel me all day." I turned the volume up loud as hell on his ass. We damn sure didn't need to hear the things him and Dree do. Let it be me or Kane talking about our woman and he cusses us out even worse.

Anyway, where we going?"

"Nigga, didn't you ask us to ride with you to see the house you had being built?"

"Oh yea. Good pussy will definitely make you lose your memory."

"I'm about to put your strung ass out."

"Like both of y'all ain't strung." Kane and I both turned our heads.

"Exactly!" For the rest of the ride we talked mad shit to each other.

After we saw SJ's house we went out to eat and ended up getting fucked up at the bar. Dree had to come get us and she talked shit to each of us until she dropped us off. I went in the house and gave Lexi some more dick and passed out. At least we both went to bed happy. I know, I did.

Lexi

I wholeheartedly understood where Frankie was coming from as far as being careful. I wasn't trying to get in drama but who really wants someone following them constantly? I know it's to keep me safe but damn. I am happy security came just as we stepped out the restaurant because the look in my aunt's eye was not a good one.

The way my mom looked at me, had me sad for a moment because I think she believes my aunt would kill her. I'm not saying she wouldn't but if she even harmed my mother, my father would be on a warpath worse than he already is.

I'm still upset it took Frankie four days to talk to me and he's only speaking to me now because I gave his ass some pussy last night. It's all good tho. I'm sure they'll be more times I make him just as upset and we'll be going through it again. Well, it won't be as bad as this.

"Hey daddy." I spoke after walking in their house. This is my first time visiting since the shit with my aunt.

PAP! He popped me on the back of the head.

"You better be lucky your mom did some nice things for me because I was coming to beat yo ass."

"Really!" I hated when he spoke of them having sex or even being nasty with one another.

"Hell yea really. Grown or not, I'll still beat your ass for doing that dumb shit." I couldn't believe he was coming for me.

"KANE!" My mom yelled.

"You better not tell her I said that." I started laughing and ran straight to my mom and told.

"Kane if you even think about putting hands on her, you're gonna have dry dick for a while." He waved her off and walked upstairs after calling me a snitch.

"Where you been?" My mom had me follow her in the kitchen. She took out some pork chops to cook and I couldn't wait to eat. She always made extra food in case Kane and I came over, which we did a lot. Then she fed Frankie, SJ and whoever else stopped by.

"Home, waiting for Frankie to talk to me." She turned around slowly and grinned.

"Did he?"

"Yea. After four days."

"Four days. He held out on you for four days? That's what your ass gets." I busted out laughing. She knew the two of us were like rabbits since we got together.

"Yes and I had to initiate it." I blew my breath. I didn't mind but I'm so used to him taking the lead, it did feel a little weird.

"Let's speak on the elephant in the room." She started seasoning the food. I spoke to my mom over the last few days but we never brought up the incident at the restaurant. When she wanted to discuss things or yell at me, she'd rather do it in person.

"First off... don't ever do that shit again." I put my head down because I was dead wrong.

"Ma. I've already heard it from.-" She cut me off.

"I don't care if a million people told you the same thing. I'm saying it now because I'm the one who would've been affected the most." I didn't say anything.

"And to find out you've been doing it for awhile is unfortunate because you really had no consideration for my well-being or your own."

"Ma, I swear it wasn't like that. I hated being followed and.-" She cut me off again.

"I DON'T GIVE A FUCK ALEXIS!" When she said my whole name, I knew she was pissed.

"I could've been shot. You could've been shot. Not only that, what if Rome were out there? We had no protection and..." She stopped and grabbed her stomach.

"You ok?" I jumped out my seat and moved closer.

"I'm fine." She spoke with an attitude and stared in my face.

"I love you to death Alexis Anderson but if you ever in your life do anything remotely as dumb as that, I will disown you." I backed up when she said it.

"April, what's wrong?" My dad ran in the kitchen and to her side.

"I'm ok Kane."

"No you're not. You can barely breathe. Lexi, what happened?" My dad snatched the phone off his clip and dialed 911. I wanted to answer but listening to her say she'll disown me, stopped any words from coming out.

"Yes, can you send an ambulance to my house. My wife was shot a while back and right now she's having trouble breathing."

"Kane, I'm ok." She tried to walk off and passed out. He caught her just in time.

"Fuck this. I'm taking her to the hospital." He lifted her up and ran out the house.

My feet were stuck in the same spot. In all the years she's been my mother, those words have never left her mouth. Did she really not love me? How could she say that? Has she been pretending all these years? I didn't know what to do.

With tears streaming down my face, I grabbed my keys and went out to my car. I knew security would follow me, so running away wouldn't work. I did the only thing I could and that was going to Dree's parents house. If anyone understood how those words hurt, it would be Dree. Jiao has never said that to her but being we're, both adopted, she'd understand.

****

"You ok? What's wrong?" Dree's mom asked when she opened the door.

"I'm ok. Is Dree here?"

"Yea. She's upstairs with lil man. Are you sure, you're ok?"

"Yes. Thanks Mrs. Puryear." I ran up the steps and in Dree's room. Her and lil man were watching a movie.

"What the fuck happened to you?" SJ said coming out the bathroom. I didn't know he was here. But then again, I wasn't paying attention to whose car is in the driveway. I just broke down crying.

"Lexi what's up?" Dree ran over.

"April passed out and my dad rushed her to the hospital."

"APRIL?" Both of then questioned me.

"Since when you call your mother by her first name?" Dree asked.

74

"Since she promised to disown me if I ever did the same shit again." Both of them got quiet. After a few seconds SJ spoke.

"Lexi, we need to get to the hospital to make sure she's ok."

"For what? If she's quick to disown me, then I don't care what happens to her." I laid right there on the floor.

"Are you serious right now?" He barked and startled me.

"Yup! Call me what you want but if she didn't wanna be my mother, then why did she take the position?"

"Lexi, I may not have been there but don't you think you're overreacting? We all know your mom and I doubt she said those words with ill intent." Dree said.

"You're right. You weren't there but how would you feel if Jiao said that to you?"

"Girl bye." She waved her hand in the air.

"I've done and said a lotta shit growing up and as my mother, she's gotten in my ass over it. Did she say mean things to my hurt my feelings? Absolutely but I know it was outta love. Lexi, I really think you should go to the hospital and speak to her about it.

"I said no. Now can I please lay down?" I stood and went over to the bed where lil man was, pulled the covers back and laid down.

"I'll be back." SJ kissed Dree and ran out.

They can say whatever they want about me but hearing April say those words cut deep and I refuse to be around her.

Frankie

"What you mean she won't come to the hospital?" I shouted to SJ in the phone. I was with Kane Jr. when his pops called and said Mrs. April passed out in the kitchen. Luckily, we were in the area so when big Kane showed up with her, we had the doctor and nurse outside waiting. You could tell by the way she looked that something was wrong.

"Man, her and my aunt got into it at the house from what she says, my aunt passed out and she ran to Dree's spot. I told her to come but she won't budge."

"FUCK!"

"I'm not sure if everything went down the way Lexi said it but bro, can you get her? My aunt is gonna want to see her."

"A'ight. I'm on my way." I walked over to big Kane and Kane Jr. Both of them looked stressed the fuck out as they should; especially with everything the family's been through.

"Is Lexi on her way?" Big Kane asked.

"Ummmm." They looked at me. I didn't wanna answer but I had no choice.

"Ummm What?" Kane Jr. asked.

"SJ said, she's refusing to come."

"WHAT?" Big Kane was fuming.

"Look. I don't know what happened but SJ said, Lexi went to Dree's house crying that Mrs. April said some harsh things to her. And because she did, Lexi isn't coming." Big Kane ran his hand over his face.

"I'll go get her."

"Nah pops. Stay here with ma. I'll get her."

"Son, I'm telling you right now that if Lexi isn't here when your mother wakes up, I'm gonna have a big problem with that."

"I know. That's why I'm going to get her. What about everyone else?" I knew he was speaking of his siblings at the house.

"It's getting late and the nanny is there. She can bring them up in the morning." Kane Jr. nodded and followed behind me out the hospital.

On the way to Dree's, I couldn't help but think what was actually said at the house to make Lexi refuse to come. Mrs. April has never made Lexi feel like she didn't come from her, nor did anyone bring it up; except the grandmother and we all know where she is. It just didn't make sense to me but I guess I'll find out sooner than later.

Kane Jr. and I parked in front of Dree's parents house and stayed in the car to smoke. I don't know about him but I needed to calm down before talking to Lexi. Lately she's been on some fuck everybody, I'll do what I want type shit. Therefore; I made it my business not to say two words to her for four days. Granted, she figured out a way to get me to speak but those four days killed her.

She tried her best to get me to talk too. She cooked all my favorite meals and of course I ate all of it. She stayed up under me whenever I came in and even took showers with me. I can admit, it was very hard to maintain my current celibate situation, with her naked in front of me but I did it.

"You ready to get your bratty ass fiancé?" Kane tossed the roach on the ground.

"Don't come for my fiancé. Especially, when she was your sister first." He and I shared a laugh on the way to the porch. By the time we reached the door, Dree had it opened.

"How's your mom?"

"I don't know yet because as usual, my sister's acting like a got damn brat and we had to come get her."

"I'm coming with y'all when you go back." She closed the door.

"How's your mom Kane?" Mrs. Puryear asked coming in from the other room.

"We're waiting on the doctor to come out."

"And how's your dad?" Her father stepped out the kitchen to ask.

"He's holding up but its taking a toll on him."

"Let him know, I'll check on him later." Kane nodded and we walked up the steps. We opened the door and Lexi was balled up on the bed. We weren't close enough to see if she were sleep or not. It didn't matter because I smacked her on the ass.

"FRANKIE!" She shouted.

"Get the fuck up." Kane Jr. said. Now had this been anyone off the street speaking to her like that, I would've already knocked them the fuck out.

"For what?" She pulled the covers over her face.

"Mommy at the hospital and..."

"Fu..." We can only assume what she was about to say because Kane literally yoked her up out the bed and held her against the wall.

"I wish the fuck you would." He was in her face.

"Really Frankie?"

"Really what? He's not hurting you and you're not in danger of losing our kid." I stood on the side of them just in case Kane lost it. I may have let him yoke her up because she deserved it but he won't hit her.

"Get off me Kane." She tried pushing him but he gripped her shirt tighter.

"I don't give a fuck about you being mad. What I do care about is you pouting like a big fucking kid when our mother is laid up in the hospital."

"She's your mother." I was at a loss for words when Lexi said that shit and so was Dree, who stood at the door with her hands covering her mouth.

"What the fuck you just say?" I saw the creases in Kane's forehead and his eyes turn into slits.

"You heard me. She's your mother and.-"

"You ungrateful, selfish bitch." He was becoming angrier and I wasn't about to let him hit her.

"Back up Kane." I pushed him away and instead of Lexi keeping her mouth shut, she kept going.

"Your mother told me, she'd disown me in a heartbeat if I did some shit like that again. So excuse me for not feeling like going to see her."

"Are you serious right now Lexi?" I asked. Not speaking about what Mrs. April said but of her not taking responsibility for almost getting them killed. I don't blame Mrs. April for saying it because it probably hurt to know the woman she raised didn't care about anyone but herself at the moment.

"Yea, she's serious Frankie and the sad part is, my mother has done any and everything for this ungrateful bitch."

"Whoa, Kane." Dree tried to step in but I shook my head no. I've come to realize when they're arguing to stay outta it because certain things need to be said. Right now, this sibling rivalry had to be done because I don't see Kane holding in anything.

"April, you know, the woman you claim isn't your mother, took on a kid that wasn't even hers at the age of two just to make sure she had a mother's love. That same woman adopted you, signed her name on your paperwork, bent over backwards to make sure everyone believed you came from her belly and this is how you repay her?"

"Kane, she said.-"

"I DONT GIVE A FUCK WHAT SHE SAID." He moved closer and I stood in between.

"DO YOU KNOW HOW MANY TIMES SHE SAID THAT SHIT TO ME FOR BOTHERING YOU GROWING UP? OR FOR BEING IN THE STREETS WHEN SHE TOLD ME NOT TO?" He started pacing.

"YOU"RE FUCKING STUPID."

"Stupid?" Lexi hated for him to call her names.

"YEA, STUPID. DON'T YOU KNOW PARENTS SAY THINGS TO TRY AND KEEP US FROM DOING THE SAME SHIT AGAIN. YOU WOULD'NT NOTICE BECAUSE YOU'RE SO HELL BENT ON DOING WHAT YOU WANT, YOU TOOK IT AS HER NOT WANTING TO BE YOUR MOTHER."

"Kane, I'm.-"

"Don't you fucking dare part your lips to apologize." He gave her the look of death.

"Is everything ok?" Dree's parents walked in.

"It is now." Kane walked to the door.

"You know Lexi, my mother as you call her, will be looking for you when she opens her eyes and what's sad is you won't be there."

"I'll go." Lexi shocked all of us with that statement.

"If you step one foot in that hospital; sister or not, I promise to knock you out like a bitch off the street."

"HOLD THE FUCK UP KANE!" Now I let him get away with some shit but he was overdoing it. Dree's father stood in between us.

84

"I get you taking up for her Frankie because she's your girl but I meant what I said about her showing up."

"Kane, you don't mean that." Mrs. Puryear said.

"I don't think anyone understands the pain and suffering my mom has gone through." I saw anger and hurt all over his face speaking on his mom.

"Ever since my mom has been a part of the Anderson family she's gone through things with my hateful grandmother, my father's ex, had five kids; excuse me four." He looked at Lexi.

"She was shot not too long ago, learned my grandmother put a hit out on her and her favorite daughter almost got her killed. That alone is a lot for anyone to handle." Lexi put her head down.

"And to make matters worse, the second my mother confronted Lexi and said something she didn't like, she turned her back on her." He looked Lexi up and down and scoffed up a laugh.

"Why don't you go dig up your crackhead ass mother and be with her? Better yet; go kill yourself and save all of us a headache." He stormed out the room.

All of us had our mouths hanging open as my fiancé stood there hysterical crying. I felt bad for the thing he said about her mother but Lexi jumped to conclusions for nothing and as Mrs. April's son, he did what any son would've and that's have his mother's back. Something Lexi always had, well used to have.

"Let me take her home."

"I wanna see her Frankie." She cried out.

"We can go tomorrow. It's getting late and.-"

"NO! I WANNA SEE HER TONIGHT! KANES GONNA TELL HER WHAT I SAID AND.-" Mrs. Puryear cut her off.

"Your brother is extremely upset Lexi but he won't tell your mom."

"How do you know? He was mad when he left."

"He's not going to mention it because he knows what you said, will hurt her and as you can tell, he's not about to let her feel any pain. But can I ask you something?" Mrs. Puryear lifted her face.

"Why on earth would you take her saying she'd disown you literally?"

"I don't know. She was upset and it made me feel like she regretted ever knowing me."

"Do you know how many times I told Dree, I'm gonna beat her ass like a bitch I didn't know because she was wilding out? Or the time I told her, she had to move out and never come back when she told us she was pregnant by the punk ass nigga? It doesn't mean I don't love her or didn't wanna be in her life." Lexi, couldn't say anything as Dree shook her head yes to the statements her mom said.

"Honey, I may not be close with your mom but I do know how much she loves her kids." She made Lexi stare at her.

"All of them." She kissed her on the cheek and stood.

"Lexi whatever demon you're fighting, you need to get rid of it. And if there isn't one, you need to figure out why you're doing things to make your family upset. April loves you and you know in your heart whether you say it out loud or not that she does." Mrs. Puryear walked out and went to check on her husband, who ran out behind Kane. This has been one hell of a night.

Lexi

Listening to Kane tell me to dig up my crackhead ass mother is probably the harshest thing he's ever said to me. He and I argue all the time and I get why Frankie didn't jump in it right away but those words were like poison. Kane knew how much I hated Erica, he knew how many times I cried about April not being my mom, he also knew about the nightmares due to Erica's man and all the other horrible things I've been through. For him to throw it in my face, hurt more than anyone could ever know.

I'm sure he's hurt and is it fair for me to be angry over the things he said? Do I have the right when I disrespected his mom? Why did I even allow myself to become so angry when it's my fault to begin with? And do I have demons to deal with like Dree's mom said?

"You were dead wrong Lexi." Dree said walking with me to Frankie's truck. He was still inside speaking to her father.

"I don't wanna hear it." I tried to walk faster and she snatched my arm.

"That's the problem Lexi. You never wanna hear it. You never wanna hear when you're wrong. You say and do what you want and everyone is supposed to be ok with it because of the horrific things you went through as a child." I'm not sure why she's tryna go off about that when we didn't even know each other then.

"Look. I'm not sure what went down at the house with your mom and I don't care. What's fucked up is she's in the hospital and you're out here acting like a spoiled brat."

"Whatever."

"Don't whatever me. How can you pretend like this shit is ok?"

"I didn't say anything was ok? I feel, how I feel and that's it."

"Lexi regardless of how upset you are or were, April is your mother. Then you disrespect her in front of Kane knowing the type of nigga he is."

"Fuck him Dree. Did you see him in there?"

"There you go again blaming someone else for shit you started."

"What?" I was getting pissed.

"How did you expect him to react Lexi? That's his mother. We all know how he is when it comes to her; including you. Did you think he'd be ok with the shit you said because it's you?"

"I didn't say that."

"Lexi, you're my girl, my sister, my best friend but you're splitting the family up with your bullshit."

"How you figure?"

"You of all people know how Mrs. April feels about the family feuding. How do you think this is going to affect your father? Or your sisters and brothers? You are his daughter and she is his wife? Do you have any idea of the predicament you put him in? Matter of fact, do you even care?" I stood there silent and wiping my eyes.

She was correct in everything she spoke about. My father loved April and his kids. Us not speaking or getting along is going to put a burden on him.

"You ready?" Frankie asked when he came out. He looked at me, then Dree and asked what happened. Instead of listening to her tell him, I sat in the truck and waited with the music turned up. I need to relax and right now, music is doing it.

"You hungry?" He closed the driver's side door and backed out the driveway.

"A little." We drove in silence and I noticed him look at his phone while we sat in the drive thru of McDonalds. I saw the message came from SJ and secretly wanted to look and see if my mom were ok but decided against it.

Frankie ordered our food and passed me the bags from the lady in the window. I slipped a few fries in my mouth and savored the moment. It felt like these were the best fries I ever had in my life. Not to mention the chicken select I dipped in the sauce.

"Don't eat my food Lexi." He pulled in front of our house and stopped before putting the code in the gate.

"You still love me Frankie?" He turned me to face him after I started staring out the window.

"I know you got a lot going on and your life seems to be spiraling outta control, but know I got you." He leaned over and placed a gentle kiss on my lips.

"I'm not going nowhere Lexi. We're in this for life." He kissed the few tears away coming down.

"I don't know what to do. Dree is right about me jumping to conclusions and not taking responsibility. Kane and my father will never forgive me. And my mom, she didn't deserve for me not to be there when her eyes opened. What's wrong with me Frankie? How could I even think that way after everything she's done for me? Am I really ungrateful and selfish?" He pressed the code and drove to the front door.

"Let's go." He came on my side and carried me in the house. I continued crying as he placed me in a warm bath and sat on the side watching me.

"You're beautiful Lexi." I looked up and blushed. He always knew what to say.

"I mean it." His two fingers lifted my chin as he got on his knees and stared in my eyes.

"I know just like everyone else how much you love Mrs. April. You were hurt and said things you didn't mean and so did your brother. But Lexi, your heart is pure. It's what made me fall even harder for you. The way you love your family, and me. You went away to school and got a Master's Degree, when most chicks out here doing whatever to get the next baller or dollar. You're about to have my baby and be my wife." He kissed my lips.

"Tonight, was tough but I'm gonna be right here and help you through it."

"What if my mom doesn't forgive me?"

"Mrs. April isn't like that. But what you need to do is speak to your father who keeps calling." He showed me his phone and sure enough it was my dad. He had been calling my phone but I sent it to voicemail. If he's contacting Frankie, it means Kane Jr. made it back and told him.

"What up?" He put my dad on speaker.

"I know my daughter is with you."

"Yea she's right here."

"Tell her she has an hour to get here because if I come get her it won't be good."

"I'll bring her." I looked at Frankie shaking my head no.

"I'm only giving her an hour because of how far y'all stay. If she's steps in here a minute later it won't be pretty." He hung up and I put my head down.

"What if my brothers there?"

"He will be and I won't let him touch you." I sucked my teeth.

"Let's be clear on what went down at Dree's." He said standing up. He reached over, grabbed the sponge and soap to wash me up.

"No nigga will ever lay hands on you, in or out my presence. However, that's your brother and yes he yoked you up but he wasn't hurting you."

"You still shouldn't have.-"

"Let me stop you right there." He finished washing me.

"The minute I saw a change in his demeanor, I stepped right in. When he called you out, I stepped in again so don't make it seem as if I'm scared of him or any other dumb reason of why things didn't pan out the way you thought they should."

"I didn't mean it like that."

"Yes you did and it's ok. Lexi, brother or not, we could've gotten it popping and were about to had Dree's pop not intervened." I know he had my back.

"Yoking you up is bad too but what you said wasn't right either. It was a quick reaction and we both know that. Am I gonna say something to him about it? Hell yea, but I also understand where he was coming from. I would've reacted the same way to my sister if she disrespected my mother, the woman who gave up her life to care for a child who wasn't hers. And that's what you need to think about on the way to the hospital because your father is gonna dig in that ass too."

"I know." He handed me a towel.

"Oh and SJ is too." He showed me a text message from him going off about what I said to Kane.

"Do me a favor though Lexi." He placed both hands on the side of my face.

"What?"

"Keep your mouth shut and stop making everything you do right, and what they do wrong."

"I don't mean to." He smiled.

"Those apologies better be good." He waited for me to get dressed and we headed over to the hospital.

Kane

"Where's your sister?" My dad asked when I made it back to the hospital. SJ, my aunt Essence and my grandfather were all there too.

"Pops, she ain't coming and honestly, it's for the best." I leaned back in the chair and rested my head on the wall.

"What you mean she ain't coming?" I sat up and stared at him. This shit was about to break him. All these years my sister has called my mother, hers and now she's claiming different because my mom said some shit she didn't like.

"She claims mommy said some foul stuff to her and there's no need to come."

"What else did she say?" My father knew it was more.

"It don't even matter."

"Tell me what else she said." He stood in front of me and it was as if everyone was waiting.

"She said fuck mommy, and that she's my mother and not hers." I heard my aunt gasp. My grandfather and SJ stood there in shock.

"Where is she?"

"I left her at Dree's spot because she almost had me and Frankie get into it."

"Why?" SJ questioned.

"Because I told her if she steps foot in this hospital, I'm gonna knock her the fuck out like a bitch off the street." My father ran his hand down his face and asked me to tell him word for word what happened.

If he wanted to hear it, its because he's about to dig in Lexi's ass. I did leave the part out about her crackhead ass mother and for good reason. My father would kill me if he knew I said that shit to her.

The doctor came out ten minutes later and told us, my mom was so stressed out, it took a toll on her body. She was dehydrated really bad, her pressure was up and down and her stomach was healing well but she still feels pain when she's stressed. I could see how pissed my dad was and so did everyone else. He looked at me and asked to talk to me privately.

"Yea."

"I don't condone you putting hands on your sister."

"Pops, she was outta pocket and.-"

"I know and trust that your mother is gonna get her and so will I. But don't ever put your hands on her again." I nodded.

"I want you to go home and relax for a while."

"I'm good dad."

"I'm about to make your sister come up here and I don't need the two of you arguing in front of your mother."

"I'm not."

"She knows how tight you two are so even with you not speaking, it will show signs something's wrong."

"Kane, are you ok?" I turned and saw Raya walking slow through the door.

"What are you doing here? You should be taking it easy." I kissed her on the cheek. I expected her to be home relaxing on the couch or something, but I appreciated her showing up.

"You said, your mom was rushed to the hospital. I wanted to make sure she was ok. How are you Mr. Anderson?"

"I'm good and thanks for coming Raya. Can you do me a favor and take him home?"

"Ummm. Ok."

"He'll tell you why in the car."

"Pops."

"I'll see you in the morning." I didn't even try to keep going. SJ was there and I knew he would tell me what happened anyway.

I said goodbye to everyone and walked out the hospital with Raya. She wasn't fully healed from the car accident but she was able to walk. Therapy started and you would think the lady was there more for me, than Raya. I mean she spent more time speaking to me, than helping my girl. I'm not sure Raya noticed but since I did, the next time she stopped by, I had to let her know. Its disrespectful as hell and if she wanted to keep a job, she better respect boundaries and her clients man.

****

"You need anything?" Raya asked making her way to the kitchen. I locked the door and plopped down on the couch.

"Nah, come here."

"One sec babe." I heard the fridge open and a few seconds later she sat next to me.

"Here." She passed me a sub and something to drink. I knew she ordered dinner for herself but I didn't know she got me something since I told her I'd be home late. Usually I'd grab something while I'm out.

"I said.-"

"I don't care what you said. You gotta eat babe. Plus, I do not want your mom thinking I'm not feeding you." I busted out laughing.

The other day my mom stopped by and Raya had just come over and was in the process of ordering. She does cook for me but this particular day we decided on take out. Anyway, my mom told her that if she planned on being in my life, she didn't care what we ate, as long as we did. Her son is a growing man and she better not see him getting skinny and sickly looking. I thought Raya was gonna cry because it did sound a little harsh the way my mom said it.

"She knows you feed me." I took a bite and didn't realize I was that hungry until I continued.

"Yea well, I hope so." She sat back on the couch and flipped the channel to one of those law and order shows. The entire time she was going off about how things were incorrect and the writers need to look into law books to obtain the right information. I knew she was smart and watching her get into the law thing turned me on.

"Come on." I finished my food, took a few sips of my drink and carried her upstairs.

"Kane, are you sure you're ok?"

"Yup. And if I'm not fully, I will be." I laid her on the bed and smiled as she bit down on her lip. This is going to be the first time we've indulged in any sexual activity since her accident and a nigga was feenin to get in that pussy.

"I love you Kane." She lifted her bottom half up as I removed her sweats and panties.

"I love you too Raya." I sat her up and took the matching sweater and bra off.

"You are so sexy to me." She covered her face with both of her hands.

"Don't do that." I pushed them away and pulled her closer to the edge of the bed.

"I was gonna fuck the shit outta you but it's been a long time so I'm gonna take it easy."

"Kane. Oh shitttttt." The first lick had her body trembling. My tongue went in and out her hole and slid up and down her pink lips. Her juices began to pour out slowly. After I stuck two fingers in and located her g-spot, she lost all control.

"Yea Raya. That looks sexy as hell. Keep cumming for me." I sucked on her clit that was now hard and ready to explode again.

"Baby, I can't take anymore. Ahhhhh fuckkkkkk." She gripped the sheet with one hand and used her other one to keep me down there as she fucked my face over and over.

"That's the best pussy I've ever tasted." I kissed up her stomach, sucked on her breasts gently and rough mixed together. I found her lips and felt her arms go around my neck.

"It's the only pussy you've ever tasted and the last." She said in a serious tone. Raya may seem nice but when it came to others, but she had a mean streak as far as other bitches coming near me. She didn't even want me in class half the time, thinking chicks would try and take me home. Jealousy looked real good on her though.

"You got that shit right. My wife will be the only one who's ever felt my mouth down below."

"Your wife?" I pecked her lips.

"Yup. You got a problem with that?" I lifted her leg and pushed my way in. You could tell it hurt but she refused to let me stop.

"No and if that's the way you ask, we're gonna need to work on that."

"Oh yea." I dug deeper and felt her nails breaking flesh on my back.

"Yesssssss. You feel so good Kane."

"You do too. Shittttt, I'm about to cum Raya." She nodded and wrapped her legs around my back.

"Got damn I needed that." My face was in the crook of her neck and I tried not to put all my weight on her.

"Me too." I kissed the side of her face and looked up to see a tear falling down her face. I jumped off and sat her up.

"What's wrong?"

"I'm just so happy that we're out in the open."

"Shit, me too." She let more tears fall down.

"You sure you're ok?"

"I'm pregnant Kane." She lifted her knees to her chest.

"How did that happen? You're on the pill and wouldn't they have known during the accident?" I started pacing the room. I wasn't mad but shocked is an understatement.

"They found out after the shit with Javier and once I moved back home, I never refilled the prescription. I was so upset about someone being in my house taping me that it didn't even cross my mind."

"Say what?"

"My mom told me when I woke up and you walked out the room with my dad."

"Oh shit. Your mom knows?" She nodded her head yes.

"Why did you wait to tell me?"

"It was so much going on and your family was dealing with your mom being shot. I just thought it was best to wait."

"But the accident."

"I know. It was so early, I guess they didn't even know. Remember we had sex the whole day before we left and I had the accident." I blew my breath in the air tryna wrap my mind around the fact I'm about to be a father. I'm happy and nervous at the same time.

"That makes you three months. Shit, you got pregnant fast."

"I know and I didn't have any symptoms so it was a shock to me too."

"What you wanna do?" I asked because neither of us were ready for a kid.

"I'm scared." I sat next to her.

"Shit, me too but we knew the risks. I'll support whatever you decide." She pulled the covers up and asked me to lay with her. How the hell did we mess up?

Raya

I respected Kane's reaction to supporting me with my decision and this child. My mom on the other hand, told me absolutely not to get rid of it. She said, it's my fault I didn't refill the prescription and the baby shouldn't suffer. I stressed finishing school and she politely told me, I had no choice for that either. I was completing school regardless and it was more than enough people in both families to help out if needed.

The only problem I had now is telling my father. He was adamant about me staying away from distractions and look. My distraction got his daughter knocked up and we haven't even been together for a year. Granted, we knew one another from high school but still.

"Guess I have to get a job to support us." Kane said and busted out laughing.

"Guess so. I ain't living in no projects either. I'll take section 8 and move into an apartment but that's as far as it goes." Kane was hysterical laughing.

"At least you ain't too bougie to ask for help."

108

"Nope and if we need food stamps, I'm going down to the welfare office with dirty clothes and a scarf on my head."

"You do know we're both staying in school, right? You can take day classes and I'll go at night."

"Awwww, baby really?"

"Hell yea. Your ass ain't gonna be walking no campus at night. If you do have to take an evening one, I'll ask my mom or your mom to watch the baby and stay in the library or something until you're finished." If I weren't already in love with him, I would be now. Who knew a man at the age of nineteen could be this romantic, caring and faithful? I'll take it though.

"Oh yea. After my therapy session tomorrow, the bitch has to go."

"Huh?"

"Don't huh me. I notice how she flirts with you while she's here. The only reason I haven't beat her ass is because I don't have the strength. But it's a matter of time before I do, so if you don't wanna deal with a half dead woman in your house, I suggest you handle it." He pulled me on top of him.

"Damn, you sexy when you're angry." I pecked his lips a few times.

"Kane, you say I'm sexy for everything." I let my lower half grind on his semi hard dick. We were supposed to be going to sleep but I doubt that's gonna happen any time soon.

"That's because you are and this juicy ass pussy makes you even sexier."

"Why is that?" I lifted myself up and navigated down his pole slow.

"Mmmmmm, because I have the perfect woman. Shittttt Raya you feel good."

"Just remember that no one is gonna make you feel as good as me either." I rocked back and forth.

Being he's my first and evidently my last, we've done everything sexually under the sun. Because he's young, I wanted to make sure to please him any way I can. I'm not saying it'll keep him from straying because a man will do what he wants. But it doesn't hurt to be so good in bed that the thought of another man getting what I give him, makes him sick.

110

He's told me plenty of times that he may have had sex with other women but none of them had him feeling as good as I do. Granted, he taught me everything I knew but browsing the internet and exploring one another helped a lot too. The sex games, toys, and porn videos we watched also helped. You have to keep it fun in the bedroom and that we do.

"Hell no."

"Sssssss. Make me cum Kane?" For the rest of the night or should I say the next few hours we went all out in the bedroom. It was definitely daylight when we fell asleep and a bitch slept very well.

****

"And what did Kane say?" My father asked when I told him about the pregnancy. I thought about holding it in but when Kane and I woke up he wanted to tell his family. I knew then my dad would find out and it's better if he heard it from me. I expected it to go a lot worse but he's very calm for some reason.

"He said, I had to stay in school. I had to take day classes and he'll take night so we can be with the baby. If I have to take a night course one of our parents can watch the baby and he'll stay on campus until I'm done. He refuses to let me be alone."

"Where are you going to live?"

"Well, I told him absolutely no projects and if we had to accept housing it would only be section 8." My mom thought the shit was hysterical, where my dad didn't find any humor in it.

I'm by no means knocking people with assistance, I just don't understand why either of them asked when we have money. I will say though, if I didn't have any I'd still only take section 8. You can move anywhere with those vouchers and people aren't always in your business.

"You do know people can't help where they love?" My dad asked.

"Yup, which is why I'm going to be a criminal and civil rights lawyer. I feel the state takes advantage of people who live in poverty or are considered low income. Therefore; they place them anywhere just to save face. I also feel like it's discrimination when landlords try and decline families with section 8. Or use their credit as to why they can't get apartments.

Daddy, do you know how many black men are incarcerated for nonviolent crimes, yet have murder sentences? It's really sad and.-" I always get excited speaking about the law. I felt like our generation is going to be the ones to change so much and I couldn't wait.

"I get it Raya. I was just making sure you weren't making fun of people with assistance."

"Never dad. Yes, we're fortunate but we could lose it all at the drop of a dime. I take nothing for granted."

"Well ok then. I'm gonna be a grandfather, my daughters gonna be a lawyer, my sons going to the NBA, the rest of my kids are still deciding what they wanna do and my wife is gonna fuck me real good tonight because I didn't flip out." My mom's mouth fell open.

"And I want it real nasty Promise." I almost peed on myself from laughing so hard. He left us sitting in the living room.

"Don't laugh Raya. I had to do some freaky things with him after I told him you were pregnant. He was so mad, I thought he was gonna kill you and Kane."

"Me?" I pointed to myself.

"Yea you. He felt you knew better and instead of sending me to tell, you should've taken him yelling and moved on." I did beg her to tell him first. I was too scared of his reaction and even though he appeared calm, I knew he was still upset.

"Sorry ma but you're the only one who can calm him down when he's irate."

"Yea well thanks to you, I'll be stuck in bed for a few days."

"Really ma?"

"Yes really. You have no idea how much he.-"

"I've heard enough." I had to stop her because she's been known to say too much.

"Did he find Javier yet?"

"No but he will."

"How do you know?"

"Because you're his daughter and he won't allow any man to pump fear in his child's heart. He's aggravated it's taken him this long but he also knows that Javier has been around long enough to know once your dad found out, he's coming for him. Your dad believes he had a hideaway planned and it's gonna take some time to figure out where he is, but he will."

"I hope it's soon. I wanna enjoy my pregnancy without being paranoid."

"You will Raya. Kane isn't about to let anything happen to you again and with a new security detail; they're too scared to mess up."

"I hope so." She came to where I was and hugged me.

"Sooooo, was he happy when you told him." She rubbed my belly and laughed when I explained how nervous he was at first. It's times like these that I missed living at home but I know for a fact now that Kane ain't having me living with no one but him.

Lexi

I stepped in the hospital room and the tension could be felt. Everyone stared at me with anger and hatred in their eyes. Frankie took my hand in his and walked towards them with me. The closer I got, the more nervous I was. My aunt Essence shook her head in disgust, SJ sucked his teeth as he typed away on his phone and my grandfather looked away. I was shocked with his reaction because I'm his favorite.

My father removed my hand from Frankie's and forced me back out the door. No one said a word and once we stepped outside, my father didn't have to say a word for me to break down. He was disappointed in me and it showed.

"I'm not going to choose between you and my wife because you each have different spots in my life." He started pacing which told me he was getting mad and trying to calm himself down. Usually he'd smoke but he couldn't here.

"You're my daughter and I'll never, ever turn my back on you but you are no longer welcomed in my house."

"What?" He stopped and stared at me.

"That woman who you claimed to be Kane's mother, raised you without knowing who I was. She didn't care about stopping her life to take care of you when I couldn't because in her eyes, you were her child. Then, you accused her of letting the guy get his hands on you that day at the mall thanks to your grandmother and even though it hurt her, she forgave you. She knew you were easily influenced and a child so she held no grudge.

All your years growing up, she nurtured and raised you into a beautiful, smart and caring woman and for what? For you to get mad over something she said and disappear. April could've died and you were at Dree's house throwing a got damn tantrum over some bullshit. I send your brother to get you, so someone would be here when she woke up and.-" He blew his breath in the air and had his hands on top of his head.

"You say fuck her, well you tried to because your brother told me what he did and then say she's only his mother. Do you hate April? I mean, I can't for the life of me understand after all these years you can disrespect her the way you did."

"Daddy, I'm sorry. I thought she regretted being my mom because of what she said."

"Has she ever in her life told you that? Better yet, has she ever made you feel like she didn't wanna be your mother?"

"No." I whispered with my head down.

"I can't hear you."

"No." I looked up at him and saw sadness in his eyes. Dree said this would have a huge impact on him and I can see it.

"Lexi, I trust Frankie to take care of you and I'll be by to see you and my grandkids. If you wanna see your siblings, send Frankie to pick them up but I meant what I said about you no longer being able to step inside my house."

"Daddy."

"Lexi your mom; excuse me April was so stressed she passed out. Never mind her pressure was up and down and she was dehydrated. I can't have you around and upsetting her again."

"How can you choose her over me?" He moved closer and placed his hands on my face.

"I don't know what's going on with you, but my daughter would know that no woman would ever compete with my kids. They have and will always come first."

"But you said I can't come to the house."

"It doesn't mean I won't see you. It means in order to keep the peace, this is what's best. I don't need you stressing her out and since you feel she's not your mother, it shouldn't be hard to stay away." He kissed my forehead and started walking to the door. I heard him yell Frankie's name.

"I don't know who you are anymore Alexis."

"It's still me daddy." I had tons of tears falling.

"Nah. My daughter would never do the things she's done over the last few days. Her family meant too much to her and she couldn't fathom life without them but now I'm not so sure she feels the same."

"What's up Mr. Anderson?" Frankie came over to me.

"Take her home please and I'll be by to see her once I know my wife is good and can come home."

"But I wanna see her." I tried to get away from Frankie but he held me tight.

"I'm gonna tell my wife everything that happened while she's still here. That way if she gets stressed out again or needs a doctor we're here. Now if she wants to see you after that, it's totally up to her." And with that, he walked through the doors with me screaming out for him.

"Let's go Lexi." He walked me to the parking lot.

"But I wanna see her. Why won't he let me see her?"

"She'll come see you when she's ready Lexi. A lot has happened and everyone wants to make sure she's good."

"But what about me?" He looked over at me when he sat in the truck.

"This time it ain't about you Lexi. Your father is in a tough situation. He has to see his daughter outside the home she's always at and deal with taking care of his wife, who's gonna be devastated when she hears what went on while she was here. Give him time Lexi. I know you think differently but this is as hard for him, as it is for you."

"How you figure?"

"She's his wife, you're his daughter. He's refusing to choose you or her, yet; he will now have to juggle his time to spend with both of you. How would you feel?"

I remained quiet for the rest of the ride and thought about everything my father said. Maybe he was right. I'm not the same Alexis and until I figure some things out on my own, it's best to stay away. It won't be hard being we live far and with me working, I'll be occupied. I just hope my mom calls me because I miss her already.

****

"Ms. Anderson, you have someone here to see you." My secretary said over the intercom.

I know people probably think I wasn't working but it was far from the truth. Yes. I was injured a few times but the person I worked for understood and actually allowed me to start from home. She even sent the computer person over to connect the system to my home network. The person showed me how to work the programs and answered all my questions.

During the time of me recuperating, Dree drove me to the job a few times for meetings and to help set up my office.

Today, is the first day I actually came in. Frankie said, it was better to get out the house and wait on my mom to contact me, otherwise; I'd drive myself crazy. He was right and even though it seemed a little weird working in an office, it felt good.

"Ok send the person in." I picked my phone up and sent a text to Frankie about what I wanted to eat. He dropped me off and said he was coming for lunch. I don't know why when he was picking me up but I'm not complaining.

I sat the phone down and looked up as my secretary walked through the door with the last person on earth I wanted to see. How the hell did he even know I worked here?

"Anything else, Ms. Anderson?"

"Yes, can you call for security to come. I'm not sure this gentleman will be here longer than five minutes and he'll most likely need an escort out." I gave him a fake smile. She left the door opened and I could hear her on the phone requesting their assistance.

Rome

"Ms. Anderson huh? I see that nigga ain't marry you yet?" I said and surveyed her office as if I belonged here. I only found her because they drove passed me and I followed. I could've gotten both of them unexpectedly but I wanted her to relay this message to her pops.

"What can I do for you Mr. Lyons?" She sat in her chair and attempted to pick the phone up.

"No need to call because I'll be gone before he gets here. I'm just stopping by to have you relay a message to your pops." She stood and pretended not to be nervous.

"I'm not telling him shit." She moved closer to me.

"I know you're upset after hearing what your father did but what would you have done if it were your child? Huh? Would you have only tortured the man and allowed him to walk free?" I thought about what she said and I probably wouldn't but so what?

"Maybe I'd be ok if your pops died too but since he's alive, it's only fair to make you suffer a loss as well."

"You know Rome, the sad part about your situation is you know your father did it and instead of saying ok and taking that loss, you're pretending to care. You didn't even know him so what's the infatuation?" She had the nerve to say.

"Oh you think I didn't wanna know him? And I have a few photos of him."

"What do you really want Rome? Is it really my father?" I snatched her by the back of her hair and tilted her head back.

"I want him and you." She swallowed hard.

"Since your man killed my kids mother in her sleep, guess who's coming for his revenge?"

"Sir, you have to go. Ms. Anderson are you ok?" The two security guys asked. I was expecting to see some old frail guy, who collected social security and was here as a volunteer but no. These dudes looked like bouncers at a club. They were huge and carried weapons. What type of company is this?

I let her go and pushed her in the seat. One of the guys pulled their weapon out and pointed it at me. I never had a chance to grab mine because the other one knocked me the fuck out. I woke up on the pavement in the back of the building with both guys standing over top of me. One kneeled down.

"If you come here again, I'll be forced to kill you on sight. Do I make myself clear?" His partner now had me lifted off the ground and standing on my feet.

"Very clear. Tell Ms. Anderson."

"We ain't telling her shit." He pushed me towards the front of the building.

"It's alright. I'll be back."

"It won't be here and we'll make sure to let the family know you've been here."

"FUCK Y'ALL!" I stuck both my fingers up and ran. Yes, it's immature but fuck that. I couldn't beat those big motherfuckers and they took my strap out my jeans so I definitely didn't have a win.

I got to my car and noticed my tires flat and my window in the back was broke. I looked around to see if I was being watched and it didn't seem like anyone was out here. Instead of making a scene, I called a tow truck company and made my way to the bus stop across the street.

"You like what I did to your car?" I turned to see the bitch Wendy that used to be friends with Crystal. I say used to because I haven't heard from her, and this bitch told me she was yanked out the bar with Frankie. It doesn't take a genius to know he got rid of her and thank goodness. Crystal was crazy as hell.

"Why you fuck up my car?"

"Because nigga, you were flaunting that bitch in my face, knowing we were having a baby."

"A baby?" I fucked her a few times because she's a grimy chick but I always strapped up.

"And before you say it, we fucked raw quite a bit when you were drunk."

I knew exactly when she was talking about because after my mom kicked me out and bounced with my kids, I started shacking up with Wendy. It was cool in the beginning until she started talking marriage and shit. This chick was desperate as hell but gave me a ton of information on that nigga SJ.

126

Evidently when he was in the hospital after Herb and a few dudes shot his truck up, she tried to kick it to him and his girl blacked out on her. Whitney's dumb ass tased Dree and SJ knocked Wendy out. Anyway, she found his information and tried to go by his house but it was burned to the ground. Crazy as it sounds, the bitch got his girls info but neither of them have been there, which didn't help me out none. I camped out there a few nights thinking they'd return for clothes or something but nope.

Now her crazy ass out here destroying my shit because she in her feelings. I guess she thought giving me the info would work in her favor. It did for the moment but I moved into a motel to get away from her and she still found me.

"Ok what you want?" I looked around to see if anyone was paying attention. You know people love to record and call the cops.

"Just for you to come home so we can be a family." I busted out laughing.

I was about to speak when a black Tahoe came flying down the street. The window opened and a machine gun, rifle or something came out. It was pointed in our direction but the aim was at her. Who the hell else did she piss off?

"GET DOWN!" I shouted but it was too late. Wendy's body shook violently as the bullets ripped through her body. I couldn't even save her if I tried. The truck stopped in front of me.

"Yo, ain't this the nigga boss man looking for?" I heard one of the guys say and took off. Bullets were flying past my ear as I ran through alleyways. There was no way I was about to get caught; especially when that Kane nigga had to go first. I'm just going after Lexi to piss her nigga off. I had to hurry up before they caught me.

SJ

"Shit Dree. I'm telling you if you weren't already pregnant, you'd be now." I said in her ear as I tried to catch my breath. The two of us were in my hotel room fucking the hell outta each other and had been all day.

"I know and I'm getting straight on birth control when I push this one out." I laid on the side of her and rested my arm on her belly. She was going on six months. Time seemed to be flying and her stomach was growing.

You would think with everything my family's gone through, years would have passed but nope. Its only been a year. Granted, she made me wait a couple of months after we started talking to sleep with me due to Whitney. But everything happens for a reason and me waiting, only made my respect for her grow and now look where we at.

"You know after I deliver, we can't have sex for a few weeks and I dare you to step out." I started laughing.

"Ain't nobody stepping out woman. Turn over." She did like I asked and rested her head on the side of her arm. I pushed some of her hair out of her face.

"You wanna marry me?" She smiled.

"SJ, what do you really want?" I shifted my shoulder weight on my elbow and stared at her.

"Dree, on some real shit; I'm done with fucking all these different women. I been there and done that. Plus, I don't see myself being with anyone else. I love you and your son and as soon as my house is finished, I was gonna ask you to move in. I figured why not get the hard part over with now and deal with the rest later? So again, will you marry me?" I reached under the bed and pulled out the velvet box to show her the eight-carat diamond ring. Lexi helped me pick it out not too long ago. I was shocked she was able to keep it a secret.

"Oh my God SJ." She sat up and wiped her face.

"I'm about to put this ring up because.-"

"Yes, baby yes." I slid it on her finger and watched her smile grow. I didn't get a kiss, hug, nothing before she snatched her phone, took a picture and sent it to her mom. I don't think ten seconds went by before it rang back.

"Yes ma. I'm so excited." She hopped off the bed naked and went in the bathroom. I heard the shower cut on.

"I don't know what colors I want yet." She went on and on speaking to her mom. I moved right past her and jumped in the shower.

"Let me call you back ma and tell daddy I'll be by to see him later. And give lil man a kiss for me." She hung the phone up and stepped in with me.

"I see someone's happy." I pulled her close.

"I am and so are my parents. SJ, I know we've been around each other for years but are you sure this is what you want?" I lifted her face.

"Dree, when you know who you want in your life, who said you had to spend forever tryna figure it out. Babe, people get used to thinking they need to be together for years before taking the big step and in some cases, it may be true. But we've basically been living with each other, we know everything about the other, your son is my dude and you have

131

me strung the fuck out. I can honestly say you're all the woman I need."

"And you're all the man I need. I love you so much baby."

"You better. Shit. That ring cost hella money." She smacked me on the side of my arm.

"How did you know which one to pick?"

"Lexi came with me."

"Well she definitely knows my style and taste." The two of them speak on the phone but haven't seen each other since the night my cousin acted like a damn fool and that was a week ago. I have yet to see or talk to her because cousin or not, she was foul as hell on all levels.

My aunt did open her eyes the next day and who do you think she asked for after seeing my uncle? Yup! She wanted to know where Lexi and Kane Jr. were because outta all the kids, they were the oldest and always around.

It took my uncle a few minutes to find the words to tell her but when he did my aunt was hysterical crying. Not only did she not believe Kane Jr. yoked her ass up but hearing Lexi

132

say she wasn't her mother hurt her the most. All my aunt April kept saying was, how could Lexi think that and she was only tryna make a point.

When Kane Jr. came in, she let his ass have it and then told him she understood. My mom cursed him out too but the main focus was Lexi and what made her even feel the way she did? My uncle said it's no excuse and Lexi don't get a pass for disrespecting his wife and family either. Yes, she's his daughter and he loved her but it's best to keep them separate and everyone agreed except April. She wanted to see Lexi but my uncle forbid it until she was better. He didn't want her to end up back in the hospital.

"Yea. Expensive."

"Whatever."

"Don't whatever me." We started kissing when my phone rang loud as hell in the other room.

"Fuck the phone." I told her when she hurried to rinse the soap off.

"It's ok babe." I turned the water off and took the towel out her hand. I guess that means no more ass for me.

****

"What up?" I said to Frankie when we met up at my parents' spot. My mom asked me to take some food over to my aunt's house. My grandfather lives there now and him or my uncle didn't want April to cook for a while. The last time she tried, she passed out so neither one of them were taking a chance.

"Shit. Lexi told me that nigga came to her job popping shit."

"Rome?"

"Yup! You know the security I hired for her, knocked him out and let his ass go."

"What the hell?"

"It was her first day and they had no idea who he was. Lexi told them next time to kill him but get this." I backed up so he could get out his truck.

"When you sent them to get Wendy, guess who she was with?"

"Don't even say it."

"They searched her house too and evidently the bitch had you and Dree information written down on paper."

"WHAT?"

"There were also some of his shit there. I'm assuming the two of them were sleeping together." I was pissed because we staked out Wendy's place for a few days because I knew Dree would want her after delivering the baby.

I was cool with it at first but listening to Frankie and Kane talk one day about not letting their women fight or get in any shit, I changed my mind. Not that I wanted my woman fighting but Wendy deserved that ass whooping my girl was planning on giving her. I said fuck it and sent some workers out to get her.

"Wasn't he sleeping with Crystal?" He nodded.

"Ain't or should I say, weren't they friends?

"Exactly. You know bitches ain't shit but ho's and tricks." He recited one of Snoop Dogg's old rap lyrics. This nigga even busted out and did the Crip dance or whatever that shit is Snoop does.

"Ma, where you at?" She didn't answer when we stepped in the house.

"Yo, let me beat yo ass real quick in this game." Frankie said to my little brother and plopped on the couch next to him. I swear between him, Kane and my uncle, those motherfuckers were addicted to that fortnite game.

I stepped in the kitchen and the persons back was to me and the look of hate plagued my mom's face. My father came strolling in slowly and had the same amount of shock on his face. When she turned around, I could've smacked her myself.

"Hey SJ!" She had the nerve to say as if we spoke.

"What the fuck you want and why you here?"

"Is that anyway to address your aunt?"

"It is when I barely know your sheisty ass. Now I'm gonna ask you again. Why the fuck are you here, when we all know my mom can't stand you and the feelings are mutual." She gave me a fake smile and stood. This is about to get real ugly.

Frankie

I was whooping SJ's brother ass in Fortnite when I heard arguing coming from the kitchen. I dropped the remote and ran in to see what was going on. Imagine my surprise when I saw SJ standing or should I saw towering over his aunt June. His pops stood in front of his mom, who was trying her hardest to break loose. His mom may have a limp but she would still get it popping.

"This my last time asking you. Why are you here? Ma, how she get in here?"

"I was trying to be the better woman and let her meet the kids but so much for that." She said and rolled her eyes.

"Well if you must know. Your dad promised me money and." We all looked at his pops.

"Hold the fuck up June. I didn't even know you were in town. Don't come in my house starting no shit."

"Stacy you promised if I need anything to come see you." SJ's dad was pissed.

"June, let's be clear on this." He stood in her face.

"The last time you were here, I told you my wife was mad for giving you more money. I also told you, don't bring your ass around my family again." I saw Mrs. Essence grin. She always said he never told his sister no but this proves he did.

"Mommy was right about you."

"Come again."

"She said, this bitch controlled you." She waved her hand at Mrs. Essence and that was it. His mom went around the island in the kitchen and started beating her ass. SJ and his pops stood there watching. I was gonna break it up but they told me not to.

"Fuck you bitch." June said and spit blood out her mouth when Mrs. Essence finally let her go.

"Fuck me. Bitch, we let you stay with us and you fucked some man in our bed. All you've ever been is a beggar. Kane gave you millions, Stacy gave you money too and all you did was blow it. They never hear from you unless you need something so hell no, I'm not ok with my husband giving you shit when you can work for a living."

"Stacy, you and Kane both have disrespectful ass women."

"Beat it June before it's too late." Stacy said. I was surprised he even said a word.

"Then, you let Kane kill our mother. How could you?"

"Kane didn't do shit. Who told you that?" Damn, his pops was defending his brother even though they didn't speak.

"I was there."

"No you weren't." SJ said. I looked at him and he shook his head no. Lexi told me what happened but never mentioned June being in the room so I was confused.

"Yes I was. I came into town a week before and stayed in the house with her. Who you think called the ambulance when she had a heart attack?" No one said a word. I don't even think they cared who called the ambulance that day.

"I left the hospital room to eat in the cafeteria and daddy was there. Mommy was alive and well when I left."

"Ok, shit happens." Mr. Anderson said and stayed in front of his wife.

"When I returned, the nurses informed me she passed away in her sleep. I asked if she had any visitors and they told me who was there. I knew you didn't do it because you were in a wheelchair but the hatred Kane had for our mom told me he's the one who did it. Therefore; I'm gonna take both of your women from you unless you pay me." She had the gun on SJ's mom who now had a few tears rolling down her face. Had she not been so close, all of us would've already gotten her.

"Too bad that nigga didn't kill Kane's wife but I'm damn sure gonna kill yours first." She pulled a gun out and pointed it at his mom.

"Fuck it! Wait right here." His dad said.

"For what?"

"I got money upstairs. Its not a lot but enough to make you leave. I'll get you more tomorrow."

"Hurry up and if you try anything funny, her ass is dead." You heard him tell the kids to go in their room and not to come out until he told them too.

"Ma, you ok?" She nodded her head yes and seconds later we heard a noise. His aunts body hit the floor. Blood poured out her forehead as SJ's dad walked down the steps placing the gun in his waist.

"You ok?" He went over to his wife, wiped her tears and she hugged him tight. Neither of us said a word. I made a call for someone to clean the mess up.

"You good?" I asked SJ.

"Yea. At least the hateful people in our family are gone." I told him I'd speak to him later and went to check on Lexi.

****

"Hey." I kissed Lexi on the lips as we sat in the doctor's office. She was nervous about stressing the baby out, due to all the nonstop drama in her family. I told her we should've come when it first happened but she refused. She said, nothing bothered her and she'd ask questions at the next appointment, which is where we're at right now.

Little does she know, I called the doctor on my own and explained in as little detail as possible what went down. She said, if my girl wasn't complaining of any pain, then she's most likely ok. I thought she would've forced me to bring her in but nope. I've been watching Lexi as much as possible even though she didn't know it.

"Do you want a girl or boy?"

"It really doesn't matter because we're gonna have a big family. Whatever you don't have this time, you'll have the next." She smacked the side of my arm and started laughing.

"Hello, you two." The doctor smiled coming in through the door. We both spoke.

"Ok. Let's see what's going on with the baby." She had the nurse bring the ultrasound machine in the room.

We found out Lexi would be three months in a week. She would've been almost due, had she not suffered a miscarriage. The doctor tried to see the sex but my baby refused to turn around. Not sure we'd be able to tell anyway but she did try.

"Ok, so I'll see you in four weeks and Alexis, the baby is doing fine but I want, no I suggest you refrain from any and all strenuous activities."

"Hold up?" I put my finger up.

"She is allowed to have sex sir. I was referring to stressing herself out, arguing or dealing with any unnecessary drama. Whatever she's dealing with, can and will affect the baby." Both of us told her we understood.

"Here's the ultrasound photo and I'll see you two in a month." She shook both of our hands and left.

"You need help." I lifted her off the bed and passed her shirt. I don't know why they made her take it off.

"Yea come here." The way she said it, was kinda seductive and I should've declined but the way my dick set up, I couldn't.

"Shit Lex." We were kissing and her hands slid in my jeans.

"Cum for me Frankie." She kept going. I grabbed the back of her neck, slid my tongue in her mouth and came in her hand and my jeans.

"Your turn." I stuck my hand in her leggings and the sound of her moaning was turning me on again.

"Ms. Anderson, I have your paperwork." The nurse said barging in. Luckily, they had one of those dividers. Otherwise; she would've gotten a shock.

"Ok thank you." Lexi peeked around the thing.

"I want more. Can we fuck in the truck?"

"We can fuck wherever you want. Hurry up." She didn't have to ask me twice. When we got outside, I pulled off and parked on a side street. I didn't wanna anyone to call the cops and they would outside a place of business.

"Ride that shit Lex." She was facing the front with her hands gripping the dashboard.

"Fuck. Fuck. Fuck. It feels so good Frankie." Needless to say, we stayed in the truck for a while getting our freak on. I was happy no old lady drove on the side of us like they did SJ. Oh well, they would've gotten a show for sure.

Dree

"Hey bitch. How you been?" I asked Lexi when I sat down at the table. She wanted to come out for lunch to talk. I wasn't gonna come at first because this baby had me feeling like I worked three jobs. I was tired as hell all the time.

"I'm good and you? Oh my God, he gave it to you." She snatched my hand and gawked over the ring.

"Heffa, he told me you picked it out." She tossed my hand away.

"Can I have my moment as your best friend? Dag." I started laughing.

"Your moment?"

"Yes Heffa. I have to be the overly excited, souped up, can't wait for the bachelorette party, matron of honor type of bitch. You just took that away with your petty ass." She picked the menu up.

"What the fuck ever. Anyway, how did the doctor's appointment go?"

"Good. The baby refused to turn over, I can't deal with anymore stress, Frankie and I had sex on a side street and I miss my mom." Tears just started flowing down her face. I put my menu down and moved closer.

"Lexi, I'm sure she misses you too." I rubbed her back.

"Then why hasn't she contacted me?"

"I really believe your dad is waiting until she's better. Lexi, the stress really did a number on her. If she sees you and gets upset, who's to say it won't happen again?"

"I know and it's selfish of me to wanna see her anyway. But she wanted to attend every doctor's appointment and..." She cried harder. I asked the waitress to come back in a few minutes.

"Look. I'll talk to SJ tonight and see if he can talk to your dad."

"I see my dad all the time with my sisters and brothers but he said it's not time yet. You think my mom is upset?" I grabbed a napkin and wiped her face.

"Even if she is, you are still her daughter."

"I am right?"

"Yes but in my opinion, before you make an attempt to see her, you should talk to Kane." She sucked her teeth.

"Be mad all you want but you were wrong. What if your other brothers and sisters were older and he told them what you did? They be just as mad."

"I guess."

"I'm telling you, he's your best bet. Plus, your mom is gonna make you two apologize and make up anyway." I shrugged my shoulders and picked my menu back up.

"Yea, I guess. Hey boo." I looked up and Raya was standing there. We each gave her a hug and offered her a seat. The waitress came back and all of us ordered.

"What you doing here?" I asked because I didn't invite her and I know Lexi didn't.

"Well. I received a text message from someone asking me to meet them here." She looked around the restaurant to see if the person was there already.

"Who?"

"Javier?"

"Who the hell is that?" Both of us asked at the same time.

"The guy who's been taping me and showed up at my doctor's appointment."

"WHAT!" Lexi and I we're both aggravated.

"Are you crazy? Does Kane know? What time is this guy supposed to come here?" I asked and started looking myself, even though I had no clue what he looked like.

"No, he doesn't. I didn't wanna tell him because he'll overreact."

"Ya think. His girl is on a dummy mission alone and the guy is coming who's been watching her. I damn sure think he's going to overreact." Lexi said.

"But you two are here." Is this chick doofy or something?

"You had no idea we were here though."

"I know right. I thought this would be a one-man show but now it's three." Lexi and I looked at each other and busted out laughing.

"Bitch, you crazy." Lexi said and picked her drink up.

"I know but Kane is going to be mad and I can't wait to have that make up sex." This chick had the nerve to shiver.

"Ugh ahh." I couldn't stop laughing.

"Oh, and I'm pregnant." She smiled and started eating as if what she said didn't matter. How the hell is she tryna get at some dude with a baby in her stomach. I sent SJ a message because even though it may be funny at the moment, if the guy does come, how are three pregnant women gonna take him down?

"Well, look who it is." We all looked up and saw Danielle. Yup, the one Herb cheated on me with, had kids with and married. I peeked around her to see if he were here. I'll kill him myself if hes with her..

"Which guy you looking for? Herb or SJ?" I stood and her mouth dropped. My stomach had a way of making people do that.

"What do you want?" I crossed my arms in front of me and she noticed the ring.

"Damn, I see he locked you down. I guess that dick is off limits." I punched her dead in the face.

149

"That dick will always be off limits bitch. SJ is my man and nothing you say can change that." Lexi pulled me back.

"Except that we're expecting." I laughed.

"You mean with Herb. SJ told me how you tried to sleep with him and he wasn't beat." It was her turn to laugh as she asked the waitress for some ice and to contact the police.

"Is that what he told you?" She smirked.

"Honey, I thought I told you it's his motive to secure the woman, then continue to play on the side. Sugar, we've slept together a few times since you've known about me."

"Bullshit!"

"Let's go Dree before you get arrested." Lexi and Raya tried to pull me away.

"I don't need to lie boo." You heard the cops coming. The waitress handed her some ice and sat her down.

"Make sure housekeeping changes those sheets in the hotel, before you go to sleep." I stopped in my tracks and turned around. Just as I was about to pound on her again, one of the cops grabbed me.

"Sir, I want her arrested for assault. Look at my face." I shook my head as her red eye began to swell.

"Ma'am you're under arrest." The cop read me my rights and placed me in the car. I saw Lexi on the phone and Raya was standing there looking petrified. I didn't see any men around her but her facial expression definitely showed something was indeed wrong.

I tried to get Lexi's attention but she was so engrossed in the phone, she paid me no mind. The cop sat in the car and asked if I were ok because I'm pregnant and he wanted to make sure I wasn't hit. I told him I was good and asked if we could wait until my fiancé showed up. I was trying to keep Raya in my view. The cop ignored me and pulled off. I turned to look back and some man was standing behind Raya with a huge smile on his face.

"FUCK! Can I use your phone?" The cop gave me a *yea right* look.

"Please. My friend is in danger."

"You can make a call at the station."

"Please. He's going to hurt her."

"You mean like you hurt that woman in the restaurant? Did you know she's pregnant and why are you fighting anyway? You're just about due." He was popping mad shit.

I couldn't even get mad because he was doing his job and he was right about me not fighting. I had no business putting my hands on her. Not only is SJ going to kill me, I hope Kane gets there in enough time to save Raya.

Raya

Watching the cops haul Dree away made me a little nervous because Javier was coming and the more people around the better. Before people start calling me dumb and stupid, let me explain why I chose to trap him this way.

When a person is after you, they'll stop at nothing to get you. I learned this after finding out about him taping and watching me for God only knows how long. I also know, if you wanna get rid of the person sometimes you'll need to come up with your own scheme, which is what I did.

Over the last couple of days Javier has been contacting me and at first, I was scared he knew where I was and coming for me. I ignored the messages until he begged me to respond. By the time I did, I had already devised my own plan to get him. The only thing is, I had to gain his trust. In doing so, I had to respond to him and even went as far as pretending to forgive him. However, it wasn't the case.

He and I text daily and come to find out, he was watching me longer than he initially said. I wasn't surprised because you don't just start when a person becomes of legal age. Anyway, he started sending me inappropriate messages and even a few videos of him jerking off. *Crazy, I know*. I never returned the favor and told him it's because I'm still inexperienced and not comfortable with it.

Long story short, he asked me to meet him and no I didn't tell Kane. The reason being, he'd probably keep me in the house and come himself. I knew if Javier spotted him and not me, the plan would backfire and I'd be living with paranoia even longer and who has time for that? I wanted to enjoy my pregnancy and he wouldn't let me if he's lurking.

I was low key happy as hell to run into Lexi and Dree. I knew neither of them would allow anything to happen to me. I also knew one, if not both would contact Frankie, SJ or Kane. It would be a matter of time before one of them arrived and hopefully it would be at the right time.

Unfortunately, some chick arrived starting drama with Dree and got her arrested. Now here I am watching the cop car pull away with Javier standing behind me. I knew it was him because of the cologne he wore. It's the same kind he had on at the doctor's office. The way Dree stared out the back window let me know she was aware he's there too.

"Lexi, I'm gonna go. Are you good here?" She was on the phone and stared behind me.

"I'm ok. I'll see you soon." She said and continued to look at Javier. I'm assuming she too knew who he was.

"Let me grab my things." I said and moved around her.

"Damn she's pretty as hell too."

"Really Javier? How you here for me, checking out another woman?" He turned me to face him.

"She can be pretty all she wants but no one is more beautiful than you." He placed a kiss on my neck. I pushed him away.

"Not in here."

"Why not?" He seemed offended. For someone on the run he was damn sure playing with fire tryna be out in the open.

"I don't know if anyone recognizes you. Are you tryna get caught?" He surveyed the restaurant.

"You're right. Let's go." I picked up my stuff and felt him hovering over me.

"I'm ready." He took my hand in his and had me follow him out some back door. I was praying Kane or someone would be out here but as luck would have it, I'm alone.

"Just breathe." I whispered to myself as he opened the car door.

Once he pulled off, the reality of it being a one man show kicked in. I pretended to dig in my purse and checked my phone. There were five missed calls from Kane, a few from my father and some from my mom. They must not have been in the same place if they're both calling me.

"A little longer and we'll be there. I can't wait to make love to you." He glanced over licking his lips.

"Me too. I'm sure it's gonna be good."

"You have no idea. I wanna eat your ass, pussy and anywhere else you let me." Sad to say, I got turned on a little reminiscing on how Kane has me running from his tongue when he does it. For me to be the only woman he's gone down on, he does a phenomenal job.

"It's whatever you want baby." I smiled and licked my lips back at him.

A few minutes later we pulled in the driveway of a small ranch house. There was a lotta land in the back and another car was in the yard. Why did he have two vehicles? He parked the car, came on my side to help me out and we walked in the house. I must say it was very nice and it smelled like he cooked.

"Make yourself comfortable, I'll be right back." I went straight in the kitchen to see what was cooking. My stomach was growling and a bitch is thirsty as hell.

I checked the crockpot and there was a roast or London broil in there with potatoes, onions and peppers. The aroma alone smelled amazing when I lifted the top. I opened the refrigerator and saw beer, soda, water, and a packed freezer. This must be where he's been staying.

"I'm ready baby." I turned around and all he had on were a pair of boxer briefs and a wife beater.

"I see." His dick was standing at attention already.

"Come here. I have a surprise." I took another sip of water and prayed someone saved me.

"What's my surprise?" He pulled me close and I could feel his dick on my pelvis.

"She is." Just as he said it, his wife walked out naked in heels. The look on her face told me she didn't wanna me here.

"Ummm, you didn't say anything about a threesome." I said nervously.

"Who the fuck cares?"

"I do Javier. Our first time together is supposed to be special."

"I get it but Raya both of you are beautiful and I can't cheat on her. The way I see it is, if she's here I'm not cheating." Is he serious?

"Javier, why are you doing this?" His wife had tears coming down her face.

"SHUT UP!" He shouted and she jumped.

"Please just let us go. Her father is going to kill the kids."

"No he won't. Hurricane doesn't murder kids."

"You have his daughter here. Do you think he's going to care? Javier please." He yanked her up by the hair.

"I told you before you're not leaving me. Now either you do this or I'm killing you."

"Javier, it's ok. We don't need her." I tried to pry his hands off her throat.

"But I wanna see her do you."

"Another time. Let's do what you planned." He finally let go and she appeared to be dead but she was breathing. He stepped over her like she was trash. I walked around and nudged her a little with my foot to get her to wake up.

"Go in my purse, grab my cell, put the code 2311 in and call my father. Give him this address. Hurry up." She could barely get up but did like I asked.

"RAYA!" He shouted.

"There's a gun in his glove compartment. I'm gonna run out and get it. Try and stall him Raya. Don't let him touch you."

"I'll try not to."

I nodded and made my way to the back. I pray she gets back in here on time. When I stepped in the room this man was spread eagle on the bed. Dick in his hand and one hand behind his head. Lord, help me.

Kane Jr.

"How much longer?" Raya's dad asked.

Lexi sent me a text telling me to get over to the restaurant because my girl was on some secret mission bullshit and might die. I didn't respond and rushed over there quickly to try and stop her. On the way, I contacted her pops and told him what happened and where to meet me.

This man came with Arnold and three black suburbans' full of niggas. I was shocked he still had people riding for him but then again, all OG's do because my dad does as well.

Anyway, SJ and Frankie pulled up at the same time. Dree got arrested and the bitch Danielle split right before we got there. SJ asked if I needed him. I told him no so he hopped in the car and rushed down to the station to get Dree. He was fuming after hearing what happened. There's no doubt in my mind he's going to kill Danielle.

"We're almost there." I looked down at my phone with the tracker. Ever since we found out about the nigga taping her,

I placed the tracker on her phone for reasons like this. Thank goodness he didn't take her phone or we'd be shit outta luck.

"Good. What the hell was Raya thinking?" He asked and I wanted to know the same thing. Frankie and his pops were in the back seat getting shut ready in case we needed heavy artillery. Oh yea, we were prepared. His phone started ringing and he answered it on speaker.

"Raya?" He questioned. I glanced at his phone and it was her number.

"No."

"Yo! Who this?"

"Ummm, I'm looking for Hurricane." Some woman spoke over the phone.

"Who the fuck is this?"

"Javier's wife."

"What? Bitch, are you working with that nigga?"

"No, no, no, no. My husband basically kidnapped me, tried to force me to have sex with Raya and choked me."

"Where the fuck is my daughter?"

"He has her in the bedroom. You have to get here fast. He's going to rape her."

"Are you at this address?" He read it off and she told him yes.

"I'm in the car looking for the gun he had in the glove compartment but it's locked. Shit, I have to run in for the keys. I'm gonna try and save her. Please hurry." The phone hung up and he tried to call back but it kept going to voicemail.

"FUCKKKKKKK!" He roared like a damn animal. I hit almost a hundred going down the highway. When we pulled up some woman came running out the house naked and straight to a car. I guess she wasn't lying about tryna get the gun.

"Yo!" I tried not to shout.

"Please don't kill me. I'm just tryna help Raya and get home to my kids." She had her hands up.

"What room are they in?" I asked.

"Somebody get her a blanket." Hurricane yelled.

"He's in the back room on the right. Hurry, I could hear her stalling but he's not going to wait much longer." Hurricane nodded and one of the guys escorted her to the truck. Frankie walked behind me, and his pops and uncle went to the back of the house.

"STOP STALLING RAYA! TAKE THEM OFF NOW!" I heard him shouting and was about to run in the back. Frankie put his finger to his lips.

"We don't know if he has a gun." He whispered and both of us crept to the back. I saw Raya about to lift her shirt and snatched her out the room.

"What the…?" He couldn't get any words out because Frankie had the gun in his mouth.

"You ok?" I had Raya in front of me. She was shaking and crying.

"What were you thinking tryna catch him by yourself? Are you crazy?"

"If I told you, you would've tried to stop me. I needed to get him Kane. I'm tired of being paranoid." I could see how much of a relief it was but it didn't excuse her not telling anyone.

"You're probably right but you should've called when you got to the restaurant. That way we could've caught him

164

before it even got this far. Raya he could've hurt or raped you."
She put her head down.

"RAYA! RAYA!" Her pops shouted and rushed in.
Him and Arnold went to make sure Javier didn't try and escape
from the back, while Frankie and I came through the house.

"You ok?" He checked her over.

"Yea. I had to daddy. It was the only way for me to live
freely." He nodded and kissed her cheek. He kept saying thank
God she was ok but her mom is going to dig in her ass too.

"Where that nigga at?" I gestured behind me with my
head. They went to get him while I walked out with Raya.

"I wanna see."

"No. You've seen enough. Let me get you home." She
tried to protest but I gave her a look. She can be mad all she
wants, but her father and uncle wouldn't allow it anyway,
either. We did hear Javier let out a loud scream. I can only
imagine how much torturing they'll do first.

****

"Hey Lexi." I heard Raya say when she opened the
door and didn't move.

"Hey. Is my brother here?"

"Nah, he's visiting your non-mother." I was being petty but so what.

"Ummm, can you give us a minute?" Raya grabbed my hand and had me follow her in the bathroom.

"What's up?" I looked in the mirror and admired the beard I started growing.

"Its been long enough Kane." I turned to look at her.

"I don't think so." She put her hands on her hips and I smiled at the small pouch peeking under her too young tank top.

"I'm serious Kane. She misses you guys hanging out."

"Too fucking bad. She should've thought of that before she disrespected my mother. You know the woman who raised her."

"Why is my man so petty?" She wrapped her arms around my neck.

"Because you love it. Mmmm." I slid my tongue in her mouth and lifted her on my waist. I let my shorts fall, slid those basketball shorts she wore over and pushed myself in.

166

"Kaneeeeee, baby we can't. Oh shitttttt." She reached behind and held on to the sink.

"If you want me to talk to her, you better fuck me back."

"You're gonna talk to her regardless or this is the last time you feel inside this warm place you love." I stopped and stared at her.

"You ain't shit."

"Nope. Now make me cum." She popped up and down, before grinding her body in a circle. She knew the shit always made me cum fast.

"Fuck Raya." She squeezed my neck and both of us came together. Now that was a damn quickie.

I let her down and grabbed some washcloths from under the sink. We washed up and walked in the room. Lexi was balled up on the couch sleep. I guess pregnancy had her down for the count. I looked at Raya and told her I'd be back. I ran upstairs, grabbed my things and went to my parents' house. Its been a few days since I've seen my mom and I wanted to ask her if I should accept Lexi's apology?

"Hey baby." She was lying on the couch and my dad had her feet on his lap.

"Sooooo, your fake daughter is at my house."

PAP! She threw the remote at me and my pops busted out laughing.

"Don't call her that."

"Well, the child your husband had is there."

"Kane, if you don't get your son." Me and my father were cracking up but she wasn't. She gave my dad a look and he cleared his throat.

"Anyway ma, she's at the house and I'm not really beat to speak to her." My mom sat up.

"Kane, I know what she said hurt all of us, but honey we have to forgive her. She was in her feelings and said some nasty things and you did too." I fell back on the chair. They still didn't know I called her mom a crackhead and told her to go kill herself.

"Regardless, if I'm her blood mother or not, she is your blood sister."

"Pops, you think she was switched at birth?" He wanted so bad to laugh but wouldn't do it in front of my mom.

"Boy, you got one more time."

"Ok. Ok ma. I guess, I'll forgive her but she better not say it again."

"I doubt she will." My pops said.

"How you know?"

"Because she regrets it. When I see her, she keeps asking to stop by but I have to make sure your mom is ok first." I heard a car pull in the driveway and stood up to check the window to see who was here.

"Well, looks like she's ready because her car just pulled in the driveway." My mom got a smile on her face and sat up. All I know is, Lexi better apologize first.

"Looks like Frankie pulled up behind her." I shook my head. Her punk ass couldn't go nowhere without him.

Lexi

"You ok?" Raya asked. I fell asleep when she went to talk to him. It was only a cat cap because I heard the front door slam.

"I'm good. Was that Kane?"

"Yea." She sat down next to me.

"I'm sorry about him leaving. Maybe you should've called first."

"Its ok. I'm gonna go try and speak to my mom now."

"You want me to go?"

"No, its probably going to get ugly; especially if my brother's there. He can be real petty and childish." She started laughing.

"You don't have to tell me. Oh, and thanks for calling or texting him to come get me." I thought they wouldn't get to her in time but I see they did.

"Of course. Plus, if I didn't he'd kick my ass for real this time."

"You sure, you don't want me to come?" She had a concerned look on her face.

"I'm sure. Lock up behind me." She gave me a hug, waited for me to get in my car and closed the door. My brother really had a good woman and she's definitely changed him for the better.

I parked in front of my parents' house and sat there. I know its going to take a lotta begging to get back in my mom's good graces. I blew my breath and picked my phone up to call Frankie.

"Hey babe. What's up?"

"How long are you gonna be?"

"We're almost done. Are you ok? Where are you?"

"I'm at my parents."

"You wanna wait for me to come?"

"I was but you're far. I may as well go ahead and get this over with." I told him.

"A'ight. I'll be there as soon as I'm done."

"Ok. Love you."

"Love you too Lexi and take a deep breath. Don't go in there getting worked up. You know the doctor said, no stress."

"I know. Hurry up home."

"I will." I blew him a kiss through the phone and opened my car door, only to have my arm yanked on and dragged out the car.

"What the hell?" I looked up and it was Rome's stupid ass. I'm not even gonna ask how he found this place. Knowing his crazy ass, he followed one of us.

"Time to get this shit over with." He smacked fire from my ass.

"Why the fuck did you hit me?"

"Just because. It felt good too." He shrugged his shoulders. I started swinging off and stopped myself when I heard Frankie's voice in my head telling me not to stress. I'm pretty sure fighting is a form of stress too.

"Bitch." He tried to punch me but I heard a noise.

CLICK! You got two seconds to put my stepsister down." I sucked my teeth because he was so got damn petty, it was ridiculous.

"This doesn't concern you and I thought you were her brother. What the hell you mean step?"

"Now that doesn't concern you. Put her down." He held me tighter. The door opened and my mom stood there with my father, who had a smile on his face.

"I see we meet again nigga." He pushed my mom in the house and closed the door. She walked to the window and opened the shade.

"That's right and I'm gonna kill her first and then you." He took something out his waist and placed it against my back.

"What are you doing?" I felt something sharp entering my body. Kane Jr. must've noticed my face and hooked off on him. My dad pulled him off and started beating the crap outta Rome. I fell on my knees and watched them take turns. My side was hurting and you could feel something dripping down my side.

"Lexi, get in here." My mom yelled and held her hand out for me to get up. I stood and limped in the house.

BOOM! BOOM! We heard and I hit the floor. My mom went to the front door. I didn't hear her scream so I'm assuming my father and brother were ok.

"Mommy." I faintly yelled. Whatever he dug in my back had me falling asleep.

"LEXI!" My mom screamed out.

"Shit! We need to get her to the hospital." I felt my body being lifted and closed my eyes. What the hell did Rome do to me?

****

"Are you ok?" My mom was lying in the bed next to me, rubbing my hair.

"What happened? Is my baby ok?"

"Rome stabbed you with some drug. The idiot was so stupid, whoever he got it from beat him for his money." My dad said.

"What you mean?"

"He injected you with fucking Nyquil. I'm guessing whoever he brought it from told him it was deadly." My dad shook his head.

174

"What was dripping down my side? I thought it was blood."

"No. He pulled the syringe out and it leaked. I have never seen a more dumb, fake, wanna be killer in my life. He's definitely his fathers' child." My mom gave him the evil eye.

"Sorry, Lexi. I didn't mean to bring him up."

"Its ok. Did the doctor say my baby was ok?"

"Yup. He's fine." My mom said.

"He?"

"Yea. While you were sleep, Frankie came in and begged the doctor to try and see what the two of you were having. When he said a boy, he hauled ass outta here and said he was going to buy cigars." She started laughing.

"Mommy, I'm so sorry for disrespecting you and saying you weren't my mom. I don't even know why I thought you would intentionally hurt me."

"Lexi, I'm going to accept your apology this time and this time only because its obvious you were going through something because of the shit you were caught up in with the security."

"Huh?"

"Don't huh me. Everybody was digging in your ass about what you did and you needed a scapegoat. You should've dealt with it and not put the blame on everyone else. You also know me saying I'll disown you wasn't to be mean because I've said it before to you and your siblings." I was so mad when she said it that it never dawned on me she used to say it to me.

"You've been away from me long enough so make sure I see you everyday." She kissed my forehead and I witnessed my dad smile. I know it was a lot for him to split his time but like he said, he'd never choose and I can honestly say he didn't.

"Did you and Kane make up?" She asked.

"No. He's waiting for me to apologize and I'm waiting for him."

"I told him about putting his hands on you. I definitely got in his ass." My dad said.

"I'm not talking about that." They both looked confused which told me Kane never told them, which made me snitching even better. He came walking through the door just as I opened my mouth.

"Kane said, I should go dig up my crackhead ass mother or go kill myself to save everyone a headache." My mom was disgusted, while my dad tried not to laugh.

"I swear to God Kane Sr. if you laugh, you'll be sleeping in the guest room for a month." My father sucked his teeth.

"KANE JR. APOLOGIZE RIGHT NOW!" My mom yelled and he gave me the evilest look. I smirked and folded my arms.

"Ma, she…"

"Now, Kane."

"I apologize but I meant what I said about you disrespecting her again. I will beat your ass." He shrugged his shoulders and sat down. My mom looked at my dad and he lifted his hands in surrender.

"He apologized April."

"Ughhhhh. Both of y'all get on my nerves." Frankie started laughing.

177

"Where's Rome?"

"Gone. That's one less person you have to worry about." Frankie said and leaned down and pecked my lips.

"Good. At least, we can live in peace." I said and snuggled under my mom. Boy did I miss her.

SJ

"I'm here to pick up my fiancé Andreeka Puryear." I told the cop at the front desk.

"You mean the nasty one who's been cursing everyone out?" I chuckled because there's no doubt in my mind Dree is doing just that.

"That's her."

"I'm glad someone is here to get her. That woman is a piece of work." He shook his head.

"She can get out on her own R & R. A court date will arrive in the mail shortly." I nodded and didn't say a word. My woman won't be in court because the other bitch won't make it there. After waiting about an hour, Dree came out cursing at the cop who held her arm.

"I don't need you to walk me out." She snatched away and rolled her eyes at me.

"Please don't ever let her get in trouble. I don't think anyone here wants to see her again."

"Fuck you. I don't wanna see none of you either." The cop had the nerve to whisper he felt bad for me behind his back. Dree is crazy but she knows when not to fuck with me. Like right now, she's trying to snatch away from my grip but once I squeezed a tad bit tighter she stopped.

"SJ, you can take me home."

"Shut yo ass up and get in." She pouted outside the door.

"Oh, you think I'm playing. Fine." I opened the back door, put the child locks on each side and forced her in the back seat. This car was too small for her and her big belly to climb the seats so I knew she had to stay back there.

"You got that bitch pregnant SJ. She told me everything." I didn't say a word and continued driving. I know, I told Dree to stop listening to outsiders. I also know ain't no bitch out here having my kids.

I drove to the spot where my guests were waiting, shut the car off and opened the door for her. She copped an attitude and stormed towards the door. For someone who had no idea where we were, she sure pretended as if she did. If she weren't pregnant, I'd let someone kidnap her ass and torture her. Not too bad though. Just enough to scare her ass. She thinks she so damn tough.

"Where are we? I'm hungry."

"How you talking shit and wanna eat?"

"Because I can. Now hurry up so I can eat and curse you out." I gave her a look and she stuck up her middle finger.

"Dree, don't make me fuck you up more than I already am."

"Excuse me." We stopped at the door.

"You in the fucking restaurant fighting some bitch for nothing." I opened the door when she stood there quiet and gently pushed her in.

The guys all spoke and asked her all types of questions about the baby. She had smiles on her face as she told them the due date, and the names we had picked out. I waited for her to finish and brought her to another door. Before we went in, I leaned her against the wall and stared in those brown eyes of hers, I loved so much.

"You are such a fucking brat."

"Whatever. How long we going to be here?"

"I don't know. You tell me." I opened the door and waited for her to step in.

"Oh shit." She covered her mouth as the flies buzzed around a half dead Herb and terrified Danielle. He was stinking because he used the bathroom on himself countless times and no one cleaned him up.

See, when we left Herb at the house Whitney burned down in, I sent a team to go by his house and wait for him to return. I knew he wasn't gonna snitch to the cops and would eventually go home for something. It took him a while but when he did, he didn't stay long and went to another spot an hour or so away. Come to find out, its where him and Danielle shacked up at with their kids. Unfortunately, I didn't kill kids and had the guys take turns in watching the house. The minute the kids were gone, we'd move right in.

The other day Herb left the house for the first time in a long time and they followed him to my parents' house. I wasn't taking any chances and had him snatched up right away. They brought him here and I beat the fuck outta him quite a few times.

I found out he was indeed one of the guys who shot up the truck me and my father were in. I only knew because one of the guys on Rome's team was in the hospital and spotted me.

He claimed not to want no parts of Rome because he brought a few of them out there and left them to fend for themselves.

Long story short, they turned their backs on him. He tried to get them to attack my uncle's house but little did he know, he had cameras everywhere and security too. It would be hard for him to get close and if you're wondering how Rome did, its because my uncle saw him on the camera and told security to let him be. They went out to get him and the rest is history. He should've left well enough alone, just like these two should've.

"Please don't kill me." Dree walked over to Danielle and hit her so hard, the chair almost flipped.

"Yo! Calm yo ass down before you go into early labor." I pulled her away just in case she wanted to hit her again.

"Where's the gun?" I took one out my waist and handed it to her.

"Please don't." Danielle screamed.

"Did you sleep with my man?" She asked Danielle.

"What?"

"Yea baby. She came in the restaurant talking about y'all had sex and the baby is yours. That's why I punched her in the face."

"Oh shit. Kill her lying ass."

"I'm sorry." She started crying.

"Is that my fiancé's baby?"

"No." Danielle put her head down and Dree splattered her brains all over the wall.

"Next." I said and she moved in front of Herb.

"Why are we killing him?"

"He's the one who had me shot and tried to kill me when I burned Whitney." She turned to look at me.

"I'm sorry baby but I'll be lil man's daddy. He has to go." She nodded and handed me the gun. I didn't think she'd be able to do it anyway. They had history and a child together.

"I'll be right out." She closed the door behind her and I ended Herb's life.

In life we have choices and its up to us to decide if we should make the right one and move on or make the wrong one and deal with the consequences. Unfortunately, both of them made the wrong choice and met their fate much earlier. I opened the door and the clean-up guys moved in to clean the mess. I grabbed my fiancé and went home.

****

"Ok, SJ. I'm sorry." Dree yelled and gripped the sheets.

"Nah. I told you to stop listening to outside people right?" She didn't answer.

"RIGHT?" I went in deeper.

"YES! Awww fuck!" She squirted all over my stomach. I held her there a little longer and fell on the side after I came.

"I love you SJ Anderson." She pulled the covers up on both of us.

"I love you to Dree." I kissed her shoulder blade and dosed off with her.

Epilogue

One year later...

Frankie and Lexi welcomed their son, who came out looking just like his father. Lexi was mad because she said, it was as if all she did was carry him. Frankie could care less because in his eyes, he had an heir. The two of them were married a month after their son was born and each of them shed tears at the altar. Lexi apologized to her mom so much, April had to threaten her in order to stop.

SJ and Dree also had their baby but she had a girl. SJ was stressed out, while Dree was in her glory. She already had a son so now she had one of each. SJ was so mad, he refused to wait until she went for the six-week checkup and got her pregnant again. Lexi said she wanted it because what happened to her getting on birth control right away? *Exactly.* Once they have this second baby, they'll be jumping the broom too.

Kane Jr. and Raya welcomed a baby boy too. April was in her glory with her two grandkids, while Hurricane was going through it. His first born had his first grandbaby. He loved them dearly but he was still tryna get over her having a boyfriend and sex. You know they say, you never grow up to your parents. In this case, she'll always be his baby. Kane on the other hand, is still petty as hell and bothers Lexi every chance he gets.

The crew would like to thank each and every reader for reading their story. Thanks so much.

A Note to My Readers

I want to say THANK YOU a million times to each and every one of you. A lot of you have been rocking with me from the very beginning. I love y'all and I am more than grateful.

For all the new readers, I love y'all too for taking a chance on a different author. I know it's hard to read and even like new material when you're stuck on specific ones. My writing may not be the same as your favorite author but I put my all into my work just the same and it's greatly appreciated to know you took a chance.

Again, this is Urban Fiction and as an author, we have the freedom to write the way we want and shouldn't be ridiculed because the book

isn't written the way you think it should be,

ended the way you wanted, or whatever reason

you can think of. However, I'm going to

continue writing and entertaining everyone to

the best of my ability.

Sending all of you a million hugs, kisses and

thanks. I hope you enjoy this series.

CPSIA information can be obtained
at www.ICGtesting.com
Printed in the USA
LVHW090216271018
595029LV00006B/325/P